Wicked Cruel

Also by Rich Wallace

Kickers series

Losing Is Not an Option

One Good Punch

Perpetual Check

Shots on Goal

Sports Camp

Wrestling Sturbridge

Wicked Cruel

RICH WALLACE

Alfred A. Knopf

New York

THIS IS A BORZOI BOOK PUBLISHED BY ALFRED A. KNOPF

This is a work of fiction. Names, characters, places, and incidents either are the product of the author's imagination or are used fictitiously. Any resemblance to actual persons, living or dead, events, or locales is entirely coincidental.

Visit us on the Web! randomhouse.com/kids

Educators and librarians, for a variety of teaching tools, visit us at RHTeachersLibrarians.com

Library of Congress Cataloging-in-Publication Data
Wallace, Rich.
Wicked cruel / Rich Wallace.
p. cm.
Summary: Three separate short stories, all set in the same New Hampshire town, explore the truth behind local urban legends as, for example, sixth-grader Jordan begins seeing a boy from his school who died of injuries after being bullied.
ISBN 978-0-375-86748-4 (trade) — ISBN 978-0-375-96748-1 (lib. bdg.) — ISBN 978-0-375-89800-6 (ebook)
[1. Folklore—New Hampshire—Fiction. 2. Supernatural—Fiction. 3. Schools— Fiction. 4. Halloween—Fiction. 5. New Hampshire—Fiction.] I. Title.
PZ7.W15877Wic 2013
[Fic]—dc23
2012042504

The text of this book is set in 12-point Goudy Old Style.

Printed in the United States of America

August 2013

10 9 8 7 6 5 4 3 2 1

First Edition

For my sons, Jonathan and Jeremy

Wicked Cruel

CONTENTS

A boy gets bullied for years before moving away. Rumors drift back to town that he died from a brain injury, caused by so many years of abuse. An urban legend? Maybe not.

Tragedy. A century ago, a team of horses drowned in a flooded brickyard, snuffed out at the height of their power. But sometimes, on dark, rainy nights, they summon all their vigor and run free.

The five children of a farming couple all died young—by accident or by murder. Over the years, the farmer built five barns on his property, burying a child beneath the floor of each and sealing the doors off with bricks. According to the legend, at least one of those children has not yet found eternal rest.

WICKED CRUEL

A boy gets bullied for years before moving away. Rumors drift back
to town that he died from a brain injury, caused by so many years of
abuse. An urban legend? Maybe not.

CHAPTER ONE

"Jordan!" my father calls. "You gotta see this."

Dad's online again, rediscovering his exciting past. Probably found a lost episode of *Seinfeld*. Ever since he stumbled on the Freewheeler website, he's been finding all these "classics" and inflicting them on me.

So I clear my laptop, then walk down the attic steps to his office.

"Check this out," he says, clicking the arrow to start a video.

I hear a piano solo, and I can tell immediately what song it is. "Another one?" I groan. "How many versions of that can you possibly watch?"

"This one's hilarious," he says, rubbing the three days' stubble on his chin.

Last night he subjected me to six different versions of the "Way Back into Love" duet from the movie *Music and Lyrics*. These were Asian recordings—from Korea, Japan, China, and who knows where else. Dad said he was investigating why the song never became a big hit in the U.S. "It's a great tune, so I'm looking to see if anybody ever recorded it here except for the sound track of the movie," he said. "Maybe we can do something with it."

These videos are pretty much all the same: Some beautiful young woman is standing onstage in a concert hall, talking to the audience in Japanese or Mandarin or whatever. She starts the song and does the first stanza, and then you hear a guy's voice singing from the shadows, and the crowd goes nuts with astonishment because he's the pop-music king of Singapore or something.

They're always singing in English, and it's obvious that the women are fluent and know what they're singing, but the men have just memorized the syllables.

The one we're watching is from a concert in Tokyo. The guy who came onstage is dressed like a hard-core American grunge rocker.

"Wow, what street cred," Dad says sarcastically. "You can tell *he's* the real thing, huh?"

I roll my eyes. The camera scans the audience—hundreds of people mouthing the English lyrics. Then I see a face that couldn't possibly be there.

Lorne Bainer.

"Stop!" I say as the camera returns to the singers. "Go back." So Dad re-hits the arrow and the video starts over.

Lorne Bainer was this incredibly annoying kid who moved away from here a couple of years ago. What would he be doing at a concert in Japan? But who else could look like that? Pale, scrawny, a long head, and that expression on his face: part "screw you," part "go ahead and hit me," and part "I'll tell the teacher if you lay a hand on me again."

The video reaches the audience scan, but there's no sign of Lorne or any other white people this time. I go, "Where is he?" and my father's like, "Where's who?" We play it again and there's still no trace. I swear he was there. We must have linked to a different version of the song or something.

Lorne was right there. Glaring at me.

"What were you looking for?" Dad asks.

"Nothing, I guess. Just thought I saw somebody I knew."

"In Japan?"

I stare at the computer screen. "In the video."

It seemed like all the guys at Franklin Pierce Elementary School beat up on Lorne. He'd get singled out in gym class whenever we played dodgeball—four, five balls flying at him from every direction. Or he'd get shoved into the wall when somebody passed him in the hallway, or smacked in the back of the head when the teacher wasn't looking. He lost way more than his share of fights after school, too.

The guys all figured he brought it on himself because of his constant whining and butting in on things. He was always defiant and stirring up trouble. I tried to leave him alone, but he was a pain to me sometimes, too.

His family moved away the summer after fifth grade. Nobody knew why, but I figured it was so he could start over with a clean slate. It wasn't likely that anybody around here would have given him a chance.

And that was the end of it. Some guys at school still get picked on and pushed around, but it's spread out more over several different kids. I've taken a bit of it myself. When Lorne was here, most of the abuse was focused on him.

I remember hoping that he would be able to start fresh somewhere else. Maybe he'd never have many friends, but at least he wouldn't be carrying this history with him. There wouldn't be daily crap from guys like Eddie Scapes or Jimmy Callas from the minute he left his house till the minute he got home after school.

I hadn't thought of him in a while, so seeing his face was jarring. He still looked the same.

He looked twisted and disturbed.

Dad shuts off the sound and some old Neil Young concert footage plays in silence. "So, you're definitely cool with this, Jordan?" he asks me for the tenth time.

"Yeah, no problem."

"This" is my parents' sudden business trip to Europe. They fly out of Logan tomorrow morning for a week. Mom's brother, David, is coming here to house-sit and keep an eye on me, since the trip was too short-notice for them to line up anyone better.

Dad is an unsuccessful "entrepreneur," and Mom is an administrator at the hospital. He usually tries something related to music or film, but this time he has an idea for marketing environmentally safe cleaning products, and he managed to score some meetings in France and Austria. Mom's going along for the ride.

The plan is that we drive to Boston tomorrow and pick up Uncle David. We'll drop my parents at the airport, and he and I will drive back to New Hampshire.

David is a "freelance" musician, which, according to Mom, means that he makes no money and isn't big on responsibility. Sort of like Dad, but even less credible.

Could be a fun week.

I get to skip school tomorrow for the ride into Boston, but we have to get up wicked early, so I head back upstairs to bed.

I sleep in the attic. This house is small, square, and old, and there are only two real bedrooms. Dad decided last month that he needed an office in the house, so he took over my second-floor bedroom and "renovated" the attic space for me. That amounted to sweeping the dust off the bare attic floorboards and replacing the broken pane of glass in the slit of a window that overlooks the street. He managed to squeeze a rickety bed frame and a mattress up the narrow stairs for me, and drilled a hole in the floor so he could run an extension cord from a power strip downstairs. I can pick up the Internet from here, so I'm set. Mom insists that I keep about a hundred blankets on my bed, but this space is actually pretty warm.

I stare at the bare beams that reach a triangular peak about three feet above my bed, then get up and look out the window for a few minutes. There's a thin layer of snow on the grass, but the streets and the sidewalk are bare. The snow's left over from Halloween, two weeks ago. It's not even winter yet.

I can't sleep, so I go over to my desk and check for messages. There's an IM on the screen from my friend Gary, just asking *wazzup jordan?* I click on it to reply, but he's already offline.

I find the Freewheeler site, type in Dad's password, and look for that video again. There are dozens of versions of the song, mostly Asian. But I can't find the one we looked at earlier. You click on one and get a list of "related videos," which either narrows the search or takes you further away. I spend an hour looking, but by then I can't keep my eyes open and I flop back into bed.

Sometime after midnight I wake up. There's a glow coming from somewhere, and I shake my head and glance at the computer screen. It's back on Freewheeler. The sound is off, but I recognize the video. It's reached the part where they scan the audience.

And there he is. Lorne Bainer. Squinting, looking smug and sour. And for a fraction of a second it seems like he's staring right at me, as if he can see me.

I turn off the power, but the screen doesn't go blank right away. It fades very slowly. Then everything goes dark.

CHAPTER TWO

It's a lot more relaxed in the house with my parents on their way to Europe. Uncle David has Mozart playing and he's chopping onions on a cutting board.

My friend Gary leans back in a kitchen chair and raises his eyebrows. "He died, you know."

"Bainer?"

"Yeah." Gary nods. He starts fidgeting with his Red Sox cap, pulling on the brim. "About a year after he moved away. He had a brain hemorrhage. From all those beatings."

"He died?"

"Yeah. One too many punches to the head."

"Get out."

Gary is even smaller than I am, but I can remember him taking a few shots at Lorne back in fifth grade. Just a shove here and there, maybe some knuckles to the jaw. The thing about Lorne is that he never fought back much, so even smaller guys knew they could pick on him. Lorne's tactic was stealthy—jab you in the arm with a pen or something, then run. He'd get caught, though, either right away or a day or two later. He always paid for his obnoxiousness.

Uncle David pulls out a chair and sits down. "Who you talking about?" he asks.

"This kid everybody used to pick on," Gary says. "He moved away and then he died."

David laughs. "Yeah," he says, "you can find a rumor like that in every town."

"It's no rumor," Gary says. "I heard it from . . . well, I don't remember where I heard it. But from somebody reliable."

David picks up his coffee mug. He made himself right at home when we got back from Boston this afternoon. We stopped at the supermarket for expensive cheese and shrimp and olives. Dad gave him a debit card for groceries.

"That's what's known as an urban legend," David says, running a hand through his long, unruly hair and tying it back in a ponytail. It's streaked with a few gray strands. "In my class it was a kid named Gerald Dibble. They said he had hairline cracks in his skull from getting beat up in junior high school. Then he moved away, and word came back that his skull had imploded and killed him."

"That sounds like what happened to Bainer," Gary says.

David gives out a snorty laugh. "I did an online search for Gerald a while back. He's an insurance salesman in Concord. Alive and well."

"Then what was Lorne doing staring me down from the computer screen last night?" I ask. "That was creepy."

David shrugs. "There's this thing deep in our psyches that thrives on guilt," he says. "People drum up these myths about somebody they picked on. Somehow, sharing the regret—'we all killed him, one whack at a time'—makes it easier to tolerate the shame. That's what the psychologists would tell you anyway."

"So you're saying I imagined that?"

"It happens, Jordan."

I reach across the table and give Gary a shove on the shoulder. "Who told you he was dead?" I ask.

"I don't know. Ask anybody. It was like six months after he moved."

Uncle David laughs again. "Urban legend."

Gary shakes his head. "This town isn't exactly urban."

"Okay—suburban legend, rural legend, same thing. Even in a dinky little town in New Hampshire. These stories crop up everywhere—the kid who drowned in some pond half a century ago that you can still hear thrashing in the water on dark, quiet nights, or the family who found a fried rat in their bucket of Kentucky Fried Chicken. It's always pinned on some supposedly credible source, like 'This really happened to my friend's aunt's accountant's brother's nephew'—some 'real' person, but never anybody you can check up on. Some of these legends have a basis in reality, but then they get twisted and exaggerated in the constant retellings. You try to investigate the origin of the story, and it disappears into a myth."

"You're forgetting one thing," I say. "I didn't know anything about Lorne being dead—or *not* being dead—before last night. That wasn't even an issue when I saw him glaring at me from the Freewheeler video."

"True," says Gary.

"So that had nothing to do with this 'shared guilt' theory of yours," I say to David. "That was no myth that woke me up last night."

I suddenly realize that me and Gary are late for basketball

practice, so I put my sneakers on in a hurry and we run the whole way there. Today's the first day. It's just a rec league at the YMCA; one practice session to get organized, then games on Saturday afternoons.

Turns out all eight guys on our team are short. We'd better run a lot because we won't be getting many rebounds.

"This should be interesting," says our coach, a guy named Steve who's a student at Cheshire Notch State College, across the street. "We'll go with a five-guard offense." He laughs, but I don't see what's so funny. This is the first basketball team I've ever been on, and I'm taking it seriously.

As we're leaving the court after practice, the next team is coming on. You can't play in this league if you made the school team, but there are some good athletes who didn't bother going out for that squad. Callas and Scapes are here. How'd they get on the same team?

"They'll tell you," Gary says.

"Tell me what?"

"About Bainer."

Callas is okay—just large and dumb—but his buddy Scapes is one of the biggest jerks in the school, taking advantage of his size to push people around. He gave Gary a bloody lip behind the bleachers at a high school football game a couple of weeks ago just because Gary made fun of his orange-and-black-checked shirt.

Gary said he'd get revenge, but that'll never happen unless he gains about forty pounds of muscle.

Gary walks over to Callas and I follow. Callas is standing on the side of the court with a basketball under his arm. He's about a foot taller than we are. He's also starting to get facial hair.

"You know about Lorne Bainer?" Gary asks.

Callas winces. "What about him?"

"He died, right?"

"I never heard that," says Callas. "How could he be dead? He's only our age."

"Kids die," Gary says.

"You're telling me he did?" Callas's eyes start flitting around the gym, like he's afraid Scapes will see him talking to us. "How?"

"From getting beat up," Gary says. "You never heard that?"

"I haven't heard nothing since he moved away."

"He died from a brain thing."

Callas shrugs, but he's looking uncomfortable. He beat up Lorne a few times, mostly with Scapes. "After he moved?"

"Yeah," Gary says, "but the damage was done here. We all contributed."

Callas holds the basketball up a bit and stares at it like it's the most fascinating thing he ever saw. Then he looks at the ceiling. "I never heard that," he repeats, very softly.

"Heard what?" Scapes has come over and he's towering above us even higher than Callas. He's got that scowly red face and his armpits stink.

"They say Bainer died," Callas tells him.

"That's bull," Scapes says, taking the basketball. "People always say stuff like that when some geek moves away. I'm sure Bainer's annoying everybody at his new school, just like he did here."

"Don't be too sure," Gary says. "He's already haunting Jordan."

I give Gary a shove. "Shut up. He's not dead."

"Bainer was indestructible," Scapes says. "Believe me, we tried." He and Callas both crack up.

We hang around for a few minutes and watch them

practice, then head for the door. Just as we're about to leave, Scapes comes running over. "Hey," he says. We stop and turn. He looks back at the basketball court, then lowers his voice. "Were you kidding around?" he says to Gary.

"No. That's what I heard."

Scapes sticks his finger in his ear and starts scratching, then stares at the floor for a few seconds. "Let me know if you hear anything," he says. "I mean . . . it would take a lot to kill a kid, wouldn't it?"

Gary shrugs. "Depends how you measure it." He makes a fist and gently punches his own jaw three or four times. "It adds up, you know?"

I follow him down the steps and out to the street. Cheshire Notch isn't all that "dinky," and technically it *is* a city. I think there's about twenty-five thousand people living here, and at least that many more who come here to work every day. Plus six thousand college students for most of the year. Main Street is wide, and both sides are busy with offices and stores and restaurants. There's manufacturing and tech stuff all around the outskirts.

I've never felt spooked in this town before, even though there are signs of death and the past everywhere. Up the street is Chase Tavern, an inn that started operating before the Revolutionary War and is said to be haunted by several ghosts. It's a museum now, and I've seen wispy lights in the upstairs windows some nights when I was sure there was nobody there.

Cheshire Notch has New England's biggest jack-o'-lantern festival in late October every year, and we make a huge deal out of Halloween, too—skeletons and ghosts all over town. And there are at least eight cemeteries here, with graves dating back to the 1700s, and very old dirt roads that wind through the woods and go nowhere.

Gary's dragging his jacket by one sleeve as we walk along Main Street toward home.

"You should put that on," I say.

"What are you, my mother? I'm hot. I sweated my butt off in basketball."

I zip my own jacket up higher. That breeze gets cold once the sun goes down.

I step around a pile of gunk on the sidewalk in front of Mario's; it looks like a wad of pizza or stromboli that got mashed under somebody's shoe. There's a diminishing line of globs of it on the next few sidewalk squares, too.

Gary stops under the overhang of the Monadnock Savings Bank and puts his jacket on. "You think somebody really found a fried rat in a bucket of chicken?" he asks.

"Beats me. I definitely heard about that fingertip somebody bit into in a Big Mac a couple of years ago."

"I thought that was in a cup of Wendy's chili."

"Whatever. It was something like that. Maybe in a burrito at Taco Bell."

"Yeah," he says. "I don't remember the details. I mean, I like to deflate hoaxes as much as the next guy, but some of these urban legends really do happen. The severed finger thing was one of them."

We start walking again and head to the crosswalk. Cars are supposed to stop for pedestrians here, but this time of day hardly anybody does. Too much of a hurry to get home from work. Finally, a pickup truck blasting Lynyrd Skynyrd screeches to a halt and the guy waves us across with his cigarette. We stand on the grassy island in the center of the street, waiting for the traffic heading the other direction to notice us and stop.

"The Bainer legend is another one," Gary says. "True, I mean. I even heard one of the teachers talking about it."

"When?"

He nods a thank-you to the car full of teenagers that's stopped to let us cross, then turns to me. "I don't know. Last year sometime."

I'm not buying this. "Which teacher?"

He shoves his hands into his pockets and looks up at a streetlight, like he's concentrating. "I think it was . . . maybe Falco . . . that bald guy who teaches sixth grade at one of the other schools. He was telling somebody else."

Right. "Real convincing," I say.

He smacks my arm. "What difference does it make who I heard it from? I *heard* it. And it was a credible source, as they say. Somebody who wouldn't be lying."

The guy who runs the Thai restaurant is standing in the doorway with his arms folded. He gives us a nod. All these food smells are going right through me and making me realize how hungry I am. Next door is another pizza place, then the bagel shop. I'd take anything from any of those places.

"What do you care so much about Bainer anyway?" Gary asks.

"I don't."

"The kid was a weasel. It was impossible to even possibly be friends with him."

"No kidding. So?"

He stops again and looks back at the pizza place. "You got any cash, Jordan?"

"Some." I've got a twenty-dollar bill in my wallet; my dad gave it to me just in case.

16

"My parents won't be home till eight o'clock," he says. "You buy me a slice?"

Uncle David is cooking up a feast at home, but I told him I didn't know when I'd get back, so I say yeah and we go to the counter and get slices. Gary shakes some dried red pepper on his. This place is tiny—mostly takeout food, but there are two booths, so we slide into one.

"You shouldn't feel guilty," Gary says as he chews.

"About what?"

"Bainer."

That strikes a bit of a nerve, but that's none of his business. "I'm not guilty of anything."

"That's what I said. You were the only one who ever came close to being his friend."

"I did not." Who's he kidding? I couldn't stand Bainer any more than anybody else. It's true that I didn't have many friends until last year, but I'm a lot different now than I was then. I was very uncool, but I changed.

"You hung with him sometimes," Gary says.

"I did *not* hang with him. Even if I wanted to—which I absolutely, positively did not want to do—then being seen with him would've gotten me beat up and ditched just as much as he was." The same fate as him: no opportunity to ever fit in.

Gary wipes his fingers across his mouth and leaves a streak of grease on his chin. "Very true," he says. "You were riding pretty close to the edge for a while. People were wondering."

"About what?"

"Whether you were more like him or us. I wouldn't have been caught dead being seen with you in fifth grade. Not when anybody thought you might be friends with Bainer."

"I wasn't." I practically spit out the words, and I can feel my face getting red. I get up to leave the restaurant.

17

He puts up both hands like a surrender, but he's grinning as we walk out. "Hey, don't sweat it," he says. "I know you're cool; I figured it out. I'm just saying . . ."

"That you did me some huge favor by becoming my friend?"

"No." He turns the corner and heads for his house. I stay with him. "Just . . . we'd see you talking to him sometimes," he says.

"I couldn't get rid of him."

"Everybody else managed to."

"Yeah, by beating him up," I say.

"That seemed like the only way."

Great solution. Cruelty.

I didn't like Bainer. You'd try to be friendly with him, or at least help him out, and he'd do something stupid in return. He was in my third-grade class and one time we were reading a story in our literature book. Each person read a paragraph out loud, then the next person in the row would read the following one. Bainer was sitting in front of me, and I could see him looking around at everybody's books to try to figure out where we were, since his turn was coming up. I stuck my arm over and put my finger on the spot in his book, so he'd be ready on time. After I'd read my paragraph, I looked up and he shot a rubber band at me from close range, hitting me in the forehead. It stung. Some thank-you, huh? I also once caught him picking his nose and wiping it under my desk.

"He was a total jerk," I say as we enter Gary's house through the back door, into the kitchen. "I'm not buying that he's dead, but I'm sure glad he doesn't live around here anymore."

The yellow lab, Barney, runs up to us, wagging his tail like crazy and licking the pizza grease on Gary's thumb. "You hungry, boy?" Gary asks. "You must be starving. Me too."

He opens a cupboard and pulls out a bag of cheese puffs.
"You're feeding him those?" I ask.

"No way. These are for me. Have some." He bends to a
lower cabinet and opens a bag of Pedigree dog food and pours
it into Barney's dish. "You never know what's in that crap," he
says, pointing to the cheese puffs. "We don't let him eat anything that isn't pure."

He takes a handful of puffs and shoves them into his
mouth, then steps over to the refrigerator and opens a giant
bottle of Mountain Dew, chugging down several gulps.

Barney finishes eating and burps. Gary grabs his floppy
ears and gently lifts them up. "Who's a good boy?" he says like
he's talking to a baby. "Who's a good little doggy?"

CHAPTER THREE

Our house smells like garlic when I walk in. Uncle David's in the kitchen with every pan sizzling.

"Pour yourself something," he says. "Something that goes with shrimp."

For him, that obviously means white wine. For me, I guess it's Sprite. I pour half a glass and top it off with orange juice.

"Smells wicked good in here," I say.

He dips a finger in the sauce on the stove and licks it. Then he dumps in a load of chopped parsley.

David's cooking beats my parents' by a factor of about a thousand to one, so he's always welcome here as far as I'm concerned.

"I remembered another good urban legend for you," he says. "This teenager is babysitting for the neighbors. She puts the kids to sleep, then goes looking around the house for a TV. She finds one in the den, but there's this full-size clown statue in the corner of the room with a creepy grin on its face, and it makes her very uncomfortable. The only other TV is in the parents' bedroom, so she calls their cell phone and asks if they'd mind if she watches TV in there because the clown statue is freaking her out. The dad says, 'Grab the kids and get out of the house! We don't have a clown statue.' The parents rush home, and when they get there the babysitter's been murdered."

"Wow," I say. "That really happened?"

"Absolutely. I think it was my friend's barber's cousin in Chicago."

We dig into the shrimp and rotini. "So," he says, "you've gotta spend a week in Boston at my place next summer. I'll show you around. Go to a couple of Sox games."

"Great," I say. David grew up here, like my mother, but he went to college in Boston and stayed there. Mom commuted to Cheshire Notch State and never left town. That's where she met my dad.

"How's basketball practice been going?" he asks.

"It's gone," I say. "This was the only one."

"One practice?"

"Yeah. It's just games every Saturday. They let you have one practice session to get organized, but they say there's not enough gym time for more than that. So today was it."

He laughs. "You'll be ready for the NBA in no time."

"We play the biggest team in the league right off the bat this weekend. The tallest guy on our team is, like, five-two."

"What are you?"

"Five even. Gary's a quarter inch shorter."

After dinner I say I'll do the dishes, but he tells me to just dump everything in the sink and he'll take care of it in the morning when I'm at school. "Let it all soak," he says.

"Sounds like a plan." I remember that I should bring in the

mail. I never get anything, but the weekly newspaper comes on Thursdays, and I usually spend about eight seconds reading everything in it that interests me.

Spike the cat is waiting on the porch to be let in when I open the door. She's very quiet and spends most of her day wandering the neighborhood. She rubs against my leg and disappears into the living room.

There's a bill from the power company, two offers for credit cards, and some supermarket circulars. The front-page headline of the *Observer* says "Mayor-Elect Promises Fiscal Responsibility."

David's in the living room with a fresh glass of wine, strumming his acoustic guitar. I take the mail into the kitchen and start flipping through the newspaper. The "Police Blotter" has a short item about one of our neighbors down the block who got arrested for a fight outside a bar. There's a write-up about the high school football team losing in the first round of the state playoffs. And the school menu for next week is highlighted by pizza on Tuesday and chicken fingers on Friday.

I look at the obituaries, which I never do, but I'm suddenly thinking about death.

Nobody I know. Two men in their eighties plus some professor at the college who retired thirty years ago. They had long lives. Wonder if they ever got beat up when they were kids?

There was this one time, midway through fifth grade.

Lorne kept bugging me about entering the school talent show with him. He had an idea that he'd win everybody over with a stand-up comedy routine, and he needed what he called a "straight man" on stage with him to set up the jokes. (Apparently, the Bainers were always watching clips of comedy teams like the Smothers Brothers or Jerry Lewis and Dean Martin— ancient stuff that you see advertised on TV infomercials.)

So Lorne had at least a marginal sense of humor. He figured we'd work up a ten-minute routine and he'd get all the laughs. Why he chose me I'll never know, but I have to admit I had a sliver of interest. My life wasn't going anywhere at the time.

So I spent maybe five minutes on the steps of the school with him, letting him make his pitch. "It's all in the timing," he says. "The straight man says something that sounds kind of logical but is really stupid if you think about it. But you don't give the audience *time* to think. Just a tiny pause for the idea to sink in, then I come in for the kill."

"And I look like an idiot."

"It's a routine," he says. "We both get the laughs. And you could use a few, you know? So you can stop being the class loser."

"Me?" I laugh. "You think I'm the class loser? You ever look in the mirror?"

"I'm trying to help you out here."

"You gotta be kidding me." Like I needed help from Bainer. The only thing he could help me do was lower my status to zero.

"So," he says, "we get onstage and you go, 'One day in kindergarten, I was making faces at the girls. The teacher tells me, "If you keep making that ugly face, it'll freeze like that forever."' Slight pause, then I go, 'Well, you can't say nobody warned you.'"

I admit that I laughed. A little.

"I heard your father is working as a plumber's assistant," he says.

"No, he isn't."

He rolls his eyes and sighs. "This is part of the routine."

"Oh."

"So . . . I heard your father is working as a plumber's assistant."

"Uh . . . yeah. That's right."

"The plumber's cell phone rang, but he was knee-deep in a problem and asked your dad to answer it. He goes, 'Hello.' The voice on the phone says, 'I need your help right away; I gotta leak in the sink.' So your father goes, 'Whattya need our help for? Just go ahead and do it.'"

So I'm laughing my butt off over that one just as Callas and Scapes get out of detention and come walking down the steps. You can imagine their reactions.

I didn't get punched out or anything, but I suffered by association. Just being seen with him would have been enough. This was worse—I'm sitting there laughing as if me and Bainer are buddies.

The next day before gym, Bainer comes up to me and asks if I've made up my mind about the talent show.

"Talk to me later," I say and start walking, getting away from him as fast as I can.

I bump right into Scapes. "So, how's your new best friend?" he says. "You guys planning a sleepover for geeks or something?"

I give Scapes a shove—big risk—and tell him to get lost. "Bainer's just pestering me like he does everybody," I say. I make a fist and hold it up. "Don't worry, he'll pay for it later."

So after gym we're walking out. Bainer hangs back and says really loud, "Hey, Jordan. You wanna come over after school and practice with me?"

Everybody starts looking at me and laughing. I stop walking. The other kids all leave the gym, and I walk over to Lorne, who's standing on the side of the basketball court. We're alone in here; the gym teacher, Mr. Brendel, is already gone.

"Shut your mouth, Bainer," I say. "I'm not doing that stupid comedy routine with you. Nobody can stand you, get it?"

To reinforce that, I give him a push, not any harder than the one I gave Scapes. His feet go out from under him, and he crashes into some metal folding chairs that are stacked against the wall.

He twists as he tries to catch himself and hits his head, but it's no big deal. There's a tiny scrape on his forehead and a drop of blood. I stand there waiting for him to start crying and threaten to kill me and run to the principal's office. But he just sits on the floor, looking stunned.

I can feel myself shaking, but I'm pretty sure he's okay. I stare at him. He stares back. So I just turn and get back to class. He shows up there in about five minutes, too. It looks like he washed the blood off in the bathroom.

"Lorne," Mrs. Munson says when we're halfway through arithmetic, "what happened to your forehead?"

I freeze.

"I got hit by a BB last night when me and my father were shooting at robins," he replies.

"Well, it's starting to bleed again," the teacher says. She writes him a pass to see the nurse. Next day there's a purplish, dime-size spot around the cut, and it lasts a few weeks before fading away.

But that was the last I thought of it.

Until now.

CHAPTER FOUR

I lean across to my desk from bed in the morning as soon as I wake up, and an IM from Gary appears on my computer screen:

ck this out. found it online

There's an attachment and I click on it. It's an obituary, dated Thursday.

LORNE BAINER, AGE 12

It says he died Tuesday, and I just stare at the screen for a few seconds and think backward. He was already dead when I saw him on that video.

I print the obit and get dressed quickly and text Gary to meet me by the bagel place. The smell of coffee and toast is coming up the stairs.

"You're not eating?" David asks as I hustle through the kitchen.

"I'll grab something out. I'm late on a project, so I gotta get in early."

"You have lunch money?"

"Yeah."

I'm out the door in a few seconds. Then I open the door again, run up the stairs and brush my teeth, and rush back to the street.

"You read this?" I call to Gary when he finally appears. I shake the printout at him.

"Of course I read it." But he grabs the corner of the paper and starts reading it again.

"It doesn't say how he died," I say.

"Oh no? That's a pretty good clue right there about the brain injury foundation. That's no coincidence."

I read the whole thing again.

> Lorne Bainer of Davenport, Pennsylvania, died Tuesday, Nov. 12. He is survived by his parents, Arnold and Leslie. He attended Lake Erie Middle School in Davenport and was a member of the city's First Presbyterian Church. He was born in Cheshire Notch, New Hampshire, and attended Franklin Pierce Elementary School there before moving to Davenport.
>
> Funeral arrangements are by the Miller Funeral Home of Davenport.
>
> Memorial contributions can be made to the Brain Injury Foundation at the University of Western Pennsylvania.

"Yeah," I say slowly. "That brain injury thing would do it."

Gary gives a halfhearted laugh, but he's looking squirmy. "Wonder which was the fatal blow."

"You mean, from somebody out in Pennsylvania?"

He shrugs. "Could be. I mean, he was probably getting beat up out there, too. He was always asking for it."

"Was he?"

Gary hesitates, scratching at his lower lip and staring at the obit. "I didn't hit him much."

"Me either."

"Scapes did more than his share."

"That's true."

"But like I said, it all added up."

"Yeah, I guess it did." I just hope nothing I did was a factor. "You said he died a *year* ago."

"Guess I was wrong. But he sure is dead now."

It's warmed up by the time we get out of school, so we take the long way home and circle toward Main Street. Neither of us mentioned Bainer's death to anyone at school, but it's all I thought about. I don't even know what homework we have or whether we've got a test coming up. I'll find out from somebody over the weekend.

"Still can't believe this," I say. My stomach is growling like crazy; no breakfast and just a couple of chicken nuggets at lunch. I couldn't eat anything. "The freakiest thing isn't that he's dead—I mean, that totally sucks for him—but that I saw him the day after he died."

Gary shrugs. "I guess his energy was still around. Something like that. They say 'rest in peace,' but how can you do that if you still have scores to settle?"

"What would he have to settle with me?"

Gary kicks at an acorn on the sidewalk and shoves his hands into the big pocket of his sweatshirt. Then he lets out his breath. "Maybe you just happened to be available. You were online, late at night . . . maybe he wanted to send you a message."

"About what?"

"I don't know. So he wouldn't be forgotten around here. Maybe so people would think twice about the consequences before smacking somebody else around."

We pass the library, the YMCA, and the newspaper office, then duck into the bagel place and stare at the drink cooler.

"You want a bagel?" I ask.

"Sure."

I order two cinnamon-raisins and Gary says he wants to hit the skateboard park. I avoid that place because a bunch of dirtbags hang out there looking for trouble. You'll find Scapes there most afternoons.

"Come on," he says. "For five minutes."

"I told my mother I wouldn't go there."

"She's in Europe."

"So? I still told her."

He doesn't even have his skateboard with him, but he goes anyway, so I walk the rest of the way alone, waiting again to cross Main Street. Cheshire Notch is the county seat. We have plenty of bars, which are filled with college kids most nights, and of course a bunch of hair places and funky stores and college buildings. Walmart and McDonald's and those other chains are out on the highway, removed from the downtown.

I sit on a bench and read the obituary again. I could show Uncle David, to prove that his urban legend idea really did come true, but I think I'll keep this to myself for now.

After dinner David says he's going down to the Shamrock Tavern for a few hours. "It's open mic night," he says, picking up his guitar. "And I ought to pay my respects at my father's old hangout." Grandpa died a long time ago. Grandma, too.

I go up to the attic. Spike is lying on my bed, purring in her sleep. I lie next to her. I'm tempted to look for that Freewheeler video again. With David out of the house I'm kind of scared to even go online, but I can't hold back. Maybe I can learn something more.

Gary's sent me another link, this one to the funeral home's "guest book" for sympathy notices. I click on it to see if anyone cared. The notes are addressed to Lorne's parents: "So sorry to hear of your loss," "Our deepest sympathies," "In our thoughts and prayers," etc. Then there's one that makes me think a little harder.

From: Ann Torre, Lake Erie Middle School

Mr. and Mrs. Bainer, please accept my deepest condolences for your loss (and ours). Lorne was in my class for only a short while, but I enjoyed his lively spirit and have missed him during his lengthy hospitalization. Please know that his classmates miss him, too. It's hard to come to terms with the death of one so young and dear, but we're soothed that his lingering distress is over and that he's found a better place in Heaven.

Whew. A "lengthy hospitalization" and "lingering distress." Sounds like his days in Pennsylvania weren't too great. I swallow hard and blink a few times, then lie on the bed and shut my eyes.

There was another time.

I'm walking up the dirt hill from the Little League field a couple of springs ago, carrying my glove and minding my own business. The game had gone well—I didn't strike out and had fielded the few balls hit my way in left field without any trouble. I had a couple of red Twizzlers that I'd tied into knots and was gnawing on them. This wasn't exactly a shortcut, but I liked climbing the rocky path and cutting through Wheeler Park on my way home. This was wilderness compared to most of Cheshire Notch.

And there's Lorne, sitting on a boulder alongside the path. I look back and see that you can watch the baseball games from up here, although the view of the field isn't great.

He jumps off the rock, right into my path. "How 'bout a bite?" he asks.

"Of what?" I know he means the Twizzlers, but no way he's putting his mouth on them. I've got them balled up in my hand and was enjoying the rubbery texture as much as the flavor, so they're all slimy from my spit. Why would anyone even want a bite of something like that unless it was your own?

He doesn't respond to that anyway. "I saw you ground out twice," he says triumphantly, as if that's such a big deal. Even the best baseball players only get hits about a third of the time. And Bainer isn't even in the league.

"Better than you," I say.

He shakes his head. "I don't think so. I play in a professional league for kids over in Boston on Saturdays. I'm leading the league in home runs."

"Sure you are." This *was* a Saturday. And Bainer had never demonstrated any athletic skill. Like anybody would pay him to play baseball.

He climbs back up on the boulder. "Let's chuck rocks," he says.

"At what?"

"Anything. Squirrels. Trees. Bet you can't hit that window."

He points down the hill to a storage shed in the lot behind the baseball field. There's one small window in the door.

"That'd be stupid," I say. "Why would you want to break a window?"

He shrugs. "Just something to do." He jumps down again and picks up a stone. "I could hit somebody in the outfield from here if I wanted to. Nobody would ever know where it came from."

I look down the hill. The players for the next game are on the field, but there's no way he could throw it even half that far.

I've had enough of him. "I'm leaving."

"Don't be a baby. Stick around."

"Get lost." I start walking.

"Come on, Jordan," he pleads. "Let's hang out together."

I don't even reply. When I'm about thirty yards away I hear a *thunk* and see a stone bounce into the woods. I doubt that he really tried to hit me with it, but he came close enough. I turn and call him a jerk.

He picks up another stone, but I know he doesn't have the guts to throw at me again.

"Put it down," I say.

"Make me."

"You think I won't?"

"You're chicken." He starts making *buck-buck* sounds.

No way I'm letting a guy like Lorne Bainer get away with that. I start running toward him. He holds his ground for a few seconds, then turns to get away. I catch him immediately and tackle him to the dirt.

"Lay off!" he cries.

I get to my knees and grab his shirt with both fists. "What'd you call me?"

He turns his head, wincing. "I didn't mean anything."

"You've got the nerve to call me a chicken?" I shake him a bit. He makes a very obvious sound in his throat as if he's gathering saliva to spit at me.

"I wouldn't try that if I was you," I say.

He spits at me anyway. I let go with my right fist and bring it back. I hesitate, and he starts crying. "Lemme go," he says.

I push him into the ground and step off him. He scurries into a ball and covers his face. "Come on, Jordan," he says. "I was fooling around."

"By throwing a rock at me?"

"It didn't hit you. I was just kidding."

"You're an idiot, Bainer. A total jerk. Stay out of my face."

He stands up and brushes off his knees, then gives me that stupid, challenging smile that I hate. He can go from crying to laughing in about a tenth of a second. "Let's hang out for the afternoon," he says. "You got any money?"

"I wouldn't hang out with you for a million dollars," I say. I start walking again, throwing the dusty remains of my Twizzlers into the brush.

That was a few months after the thing in gym class when his forehead hit the chairs. Right before the Bainers moved out of state.

Spike yowls suddenly and runs downstairs. I look over at the computer screen and catch a glimpse of Bainer's face. Just a split second, but it's him, glaring at me before the screen goes blank.

I hit the space bar and the screen lights up, but it's just my desktop—not Bainer. But he was there, right? He was.

Or maybe I'm imagining things, just a vivid memory playing tricks on me.

One thing's for sure. I'm not staying in this house alone.

*　　*　　*

The Shamrock is off Railroad Square, half a block in from Main Street, and Dad says it's one of the quieter downtown bars. That's because it's mostly older people; not enough action for the college crowd, I suppose. I've never been in any of the bars, of course, but you hear stories.

It's raining very lightly, but it's still fairly warm. There are small piles of dirty snow here and there, but most of it's melted away. The streets are quiet. The alley you take to the Shamrock is dark, but there's plenty of light coming from Main.

I can see Uncle David sitting at the bar with a mug of beer, but he's turned away from the front window, talking to somebody on the next bar stool. I take a seat on a bench under the awning and wait for him to come out. Could be a while.

A police car goes by on Main with its lights flashing but no siren. An older man in a green Celtics cap walks a black Labrador past. Soon two scruffy guys who might be students come walking up.

"Hey," one of them says to me as he reaches for the door. "You get kicked out?" He laughs.

"Could you tell my uncle to come out here?" I ask.

"Sure. Which one is he?"

"He's sitting at the bar. Argyle sweater-vest. Ponytail."

"Shouldn't be hard to find."

David comes out a few minutes later and lights a cigarette. "What's up, Jordan?" he asks.

"Just wondered if you'd be coming home soon."

"Pretty soon." He looks back through the window. "They asked me to play another set and I just got a fresh beer. . . . I'll be home by midnight."

"Okay."

"Maybe sooner," he says. He digs into his pocket and pulls

out a couple of dollar bills. "The Citgo's open, right? Get yourself a candy bar. Tomorrow's Saturday; you can stay up tonight. Watch TV till I get home, okay?"

"I guess." I grab the bills. He takes a drag on his cigarette and flicks the rest of it toward the gutter, then goes back into the bar.

I start thinking about where I can kill a few hours till he gets home and still keep my eye on Main Street in case he leaves the bar early. Brewbakers Coffee Shop stays open until midnight on weekends. I can get a hot chocolate and sit by the big front window. With the two dollars David gave me and some of my own, I should be able to pay my way and not get told to leave.

There are two guys at a table near the back of the very narrow café, huddled over a laptop. The only other customer is a balding man in a black Star Wars T-shirt that's too small for him. He also has a laptop, and the coffee he's drinking is in a paper Dunkin' Donuts cup.

The skinny college kid behind the counter looks bored and sullen when I walk in, but he perks up when I come over. "Help ya?" he asks. His shirt says Cheshire Notch Cross-Country.

"Could I get a hot chocolate? For here."

He nods and turns to make it. It's kind of dark in here. Folky rock music is playing from somewhere, but I can't identify it. This place has a hippie vibe to it, like much of the downtown: organic coffee, grainy homemade breads. I take off my jacket and drape it over one of the chairs by the window, and sit at a wobbly table the size of a garbage can lid.

The ceiling is old tin, and the wood floors are scuffed and wide-paneled. There's about a dozen of these little tables; the walls have posters that say things like, THE DOORS—FILLMORE EAST—MARCH 22, 1968 or OPEN POETRY NIGHT, SUNDAYS 6 P.M.

The guy comes over with my hot chocolate in a ceramic mug. "You all right?" he asks.

"Yeah. I'm supposed to meet my uncle here, but I'm way early. I might be hanging around for an hour or so."

"Cool with me," he says. He sits across from the Star Wars guy and they start talking about video games.

There's a rumpled *Boston Globe* on a table, so I skim the sports section. Before long the wind picks up and the rain, too, and it starts driving against the window. Nobody comes in for a long time.

When I reach the bottom of the hot chocolate, there's a quarter inch of gooey chocolate syrup, too thick to drink. So I get a wooden stirrer and eat it like ice cream.

By 10:30 I'm feeling antsy and figuring that I ought to buy something else, even though the other three guys are still here and they haven't bought anything since I arrived. An older couple comes in, shaking off the rain, and they order decaf coffees to go. I get on line behind them, keeping an eye on the street. Every once in a while groups of college students have walked past, but there's been no sign of David.

I get a blueberry muffin and a couple of napkins and go back to my table. I'm getting tired, but I know I couldn't possibly sleep if I went home. Maybe if David's in the house, but definitely not if I'm alone. I have to decide where to sleep, too. He's got the couch, so I'll probably sleep on top of my parents' bedspread. (I don't want to mess up the bed and have them think I was scared to be in the attic.) No way I'm going back up there yet. Not a chance.

Bainer's dead. How is he doing this?

By 11:30 the clerk is sweeping the floor and I'm the only customer. No sign of my uncle, of course. I get up and leave.

I walk past the Shamrock again. There are more people in there and the music is penetrating through the walls— AC/DC, I'm pretty sure. I still have a clear view of the bar. David has a full beer. He's pumping his shoulders to the music, and the woman sitting next to him is laughing about something.

I guess I can sleep on the couch till he gets home.

I take the side streets to avoid attention from the cops, since it's coming up on midnight. There's a loud party going on at one of the college rental houses; people are sitting on the roof above the front porch. The wet sidewalk in front of the house is shiny with bits of broken glass.

Our house is only a few blocks from the college, but we're in a quiet neighborhood. No rooming houses on our street. It's a dead end with only a dozen houses backing into a wooded wetlands area.

There weren't any lights on when I fled the house earlier, so I turn on every one as I make my way around downstairs. I also turn on the TV; my dad had it tuned to one of the ESPN channels, so it's showing a poker tournament. I'm soaked from the rain and all of my clothes are upstairs. So . . .

I grab a flashlight from a kitchen drawer crammed with masking tape, rubber bands, toothpicks, and batteries, and make my way up. Every step creaks. I get some light from the second-floor hallway, but the stairway to the attic isn't lit. The only light in my "bedroom" is a lamp on a table on the other side of my bed, so most nights I feel my way up the stairs, climb onto the bed, and reach over to the lamp. Usually it's no problem. Tonight I want the flashlight.

The attic is pitch-black. I stop halfway and listen hard. Then I inch the rest of the way up and shine the light on the bed. I see a slow movement, a slithery sort of rising. The beam catches two eyes.

"Spike," I say, letting out my breath. "Come downstairs with me."

The cat rushes past me and I can hear her going all the way down to the living room. I pull off my shirt and pants and grab some dry things, then shine the light around the attic, into the corners and under the bed. Nothing.

But then I hear a high-pitched ringing and a couple of beeps—my computer turning on. The screen flashes and I back slowly out of the room. My stomach clenches as I hear the opening notes of "Way Back into Love," and I move as fast as I can down the two flights of stairs and out the front door.

CHAPTER FIVE

The doorbell rings about six times and I lift my head and try to focus. I can smell coffee, and the sunlight is coming through my parents' bedroom window.

I sat on the porch last night until I finally saw David coming home close to two. Then I lay awake for at least a couple of hours after that, freezing up with every rattle in the pipes or scrape of a branch against the house. I fell asleep fully dressed—sneakers even—and pulled my mother's bathrobe over me when I got cold instead of getting under the covers.

All seems peaceful now. David's answering the door and Gary's saying, "Where is he? The game's in fifteen minutes."

"I'm coming!" I yell, and head for the attic stairs. It's daytime; safe.

My basketball shorts are hanging from a nail above my bed, where I put them after practice the other day. We're supposed to be given our jerseys before the game.

I hustle down to the kitchen. It's 9:30, so Gary's exaggerating: we've got half an hour. I grab a banana and my jacket and we head out. The morning is gray and damp.

"You woulda missed the game," Gary says.

"I was up all night."

"What? Because of Bainer?"

"Mostly, yeah. My uncle went out last night and weird things kept happening. This is getting bad."

"You should chill, Jordan. If anybody should feel guilty, it's Scapes. I told him about it yesterday at the skate park."

"What'd he say?"

"He didn't believe it. I brought a copy of that obituary with me today, though. I'll shove it right in his stupid face."

We cross Main, and Gary starts jogging. "I don't wanna be late," he says. "We'd wind up sitting the bench."

We start walking again as we get near the Y. Gary's been rubbing his arm. "He sucker punched me."

"Scapes?"

"Yeah. After I told him about Bainer definitely being dead. I'm walking away and he whacks me in the bicep."

"Hurt?"

"Yeah, it hurt. I got a big frickin' bruise and everything."

"Well, you went asking for it."

"How?"

"You go to the skate park and confront him—what do you expect? When you walk into his territory like that, he's gonna pound you."

"Yeah, well, he'll pay for it. Wait'll he sees this obit. He'll crap his pants."

Incredibly, we aren't the last ones from our team to show up, we're the first.

"Where is everybody?" our coach asks. "It's ten to ten."

Four of our guys walk into the gym at that point. Coach shakes his head and starts pawing through a box of yellow T-shirts. He hands me one with a black number 3.

"Go shoot some layups," he says. "Two lines. Crisp passes."

Gary's already down at the other end of the court, showing Scapes the obituary. I watch for Scapes's reaction and I get hit in the butt with a basketball.

"Right on target," says Louie Kulik, laughing. He's our tallest guy but probably also the weakest.

I scoop up the ball and dribble in, making a clean layup and getting my own rebound. Gary's running back toward us so I flip the ball to him.

"What'd Scapes say?" I ask.

Gary shrugs. "Not much. He was kind of stunned, I think."

I look over at the other team's bench. Scapes is sitting next to Callas, talking. They're wearing their blue team shirts, and Scapes has a white headband.

"We'll exploit that," Gary says. "Keep him thinking about it the whole game."

I glance at Gary's arm and I see the bruise, about the width of a golf ball and the shade of a purple grape.

All five of their starters are taller than all five of ours, but we're quicker and get out to an early lead. I hit a long jumper from the corner just as the first quarter ends, and we run to the bench with a 12–7 advantage. Scapes has three fouls and seemed to grow more agitated but less aggressive after every whistle. I heard Gary mutter Bainer's name to him at least twice.

Me and Gary get taken out late in the second quarter, and I realize how starving I am. "Can I get a drink?" I ask the coach.

He's watching the game intently and seems startled when I ask. "Sure, sure," he says, flicking his hand toward the water fountain. I leave the gym and go out to the lobby, where there's a charity bake sale set up. I get two chocolate cupcakes with pink icing for a dollar and eat them as fast as I can.

The scoreboard shows less than a minute when I get back to the bench.

"What'd you do, fall in?" Gary asks.

"I was eating," I say. "All I had this morning was that banana."

"Scapes hasn't played since the first quarter," he says with a smirk. "I think he's shook up."

"Yeah, well, so am I," I say.

Without us in there, Callas and the others have fought back and taken the lead. "No worry," Gary says. "We'll get it done."

The score goes back and forth in the second half, but we're clinging to a one-point lead down the stretch. I'm dribbling outside the arc, watching my teammates scramble around cluelessly, trying to get open. "Set some picks!" I yell, and Gary finally steps out to the foul line and plants his feet. I break toward the basket, slicing as close to Gary as I can so my defender will get screened. Scapes steps up and tries to block my shot. He misses, but so does the shot, and Scapes barrels into me and knocks me to the floor.

The whistle blows. That's his fourth foul. One more and he's out. But the clock shows only twelve seconds left as I take the ball for the free throws. If I can hit them both, it'll all but seal the win.

I let out my breath and eye the rim, dribble twice, then shoot. The ball bonks off the back of the rim and goes straight up, then swooshes through the net.

My teammates clap and shout, "One more!" But my second shot rolls out and Callas grabs the rebound. He whips the ball up the court, and Gary and another guy are chasing after it. Gary deflects the ball and it rolls out of bounds.

Seven seconds left. We pack into the key, shoving and grunting while waiting for the ball to be thrown in.

Gary is leaning into Scapes, arms up. "Watch those elbows," Gary says. "Don't go killing anybody else."

"Shut up," Scapes says.

"Don't want another Bainer on your conscience."

"Shut *up!*" Scapes yells, and he shoves Gary back about six feet.

The whistle blows. Technical foul on Scapes. He's out. Our ball.

Game over.

Gary runs to the bench with his fist up, yelling, "Yeah!" The coach and the rest of the team are celebrating, too, but I just walk to the bleachers and take a seat. Across the way, the other coach has his players huddled up around him. Scapes is staring at the floor, looking pale.

"We have the one o'clock game next Saturday," Coach says. "Try to do some shooting during the week. Good job today."

I pick up my clothes and walk slowly to the dingy locker room to change out of my wet T-shirt and shorts. But I just sit on a bench for a few minutes and stare at the lockers.

Scapes comes in and gives me a nod. "Nice game," he says.

"You too."

"My head wasn't in it."

He sits on the end of the bench and pushes a locker closed with his foot. "It's true, huh?" he asks softly.

I peel off my shirt and ball it up. "Looks that way." I shake my head. "Weird. I was just . . . I was thinking about Bainer right before I heard. Like he was trying to contact me, you know? I hadn't thought about him in a year, at least."

43

Scapes sits there with his mouth hanging open. He takes off the headband and wrings it out, making a little puddle on the cement floor. "You think, uh . . . you think somebody could get in trouble over that?"

"Because of hurting him? Way back then?"

He wipes his mouth with a fist. "Just wondering," he says, real low.

I wouldn't know about that. How could anybody trace Bainer's death back to one particular punch or shove or blow to the head? "How could they say that one guy was more responsible than a dozen others?" I ask. "Too many guys participated. . . . It was just one of those things." I feel numb all over when I say it. I start shaking.

Scapes closes his eyes and puts his head in his hands. Then he gets up and walks really fast toward the bathroom. I hear a stall slam shut and then I hear him puking.

Gary and Kulik barge into the locker room, laughing and yelling. "We kicked their butts," Gary says.

"They were big guys, too," Kulik says.

"Big wussies," Gary says. "I took Scapes completely out of his game. He was scared to death."

I stare at Gary until his eyes lock on mine. I jerk my head toward the bathroom. "He's right in there," I say.

"Good." He raises his voice again. "Hey, Scapes. Great game! Five fouls in what, about three minutes of playing time? Nice contribution." He smacks hands with Kulik and laughs.

"I'd watch my mouth if I were you," I say.

Gary sneers. "I don't think I have much to worry about. Scapes has one foot in Hell already!" He laughs again. "If he hurts somebody else, it'll seal his fate for eternity."

We leave the Y before Scapes comes out of the bathroom, but Gary keeps jabbering about the game and how he shut Scapes up and shut him down.

"Why don't *you* shut up, Gary," I finally say. "A kid died, you know? That isn't exactly worth celebrating."

CHAPTER SIX

I mix Cheerios and Froot Loops in a giant bowl before I realize that we're out of milk. Uncle David must have heard me banging around, because he calls, "You hungry?" from the living room.

"Yeah."

"I can make you anything you want for lunch." He enters the kitchen and opens the refrigerator. "You want scrambled eggs? A hamburger? I was planning some roasted chicken for dinner, but that's a long ways off."

"I was just gonna eat cereal, but the milk's gone."

"I put the last of it in my coffee this morning, but there was only about six drops. You want to go get some?"

"Yeah, but I'm starving now." I reach into the cold-cut drawer and find a few slices of turkey. They're a little slimy, but they smell only the slightest bit rank. I roll them up and take a bite and say I'm going to the Citgo for milk.

"I'll go with you," David says. "I could use a walk."

From the end of our street you can turn left and walk half

a block up to Main, or right and walk half a block to Adams, which is quieter but loops around and meets Main way down by the post office and the Citgo. We take Adams, which has no sidewalk, and scuff through piles of soggy maple leaves near the gutter. The sun's come out and it feels warm on my face.

"You expected to get clobbered this morning," he says.

"Yeah, but we didn't."

"You must be better than you thought."

"We're okay. It was a strange game. Their best player was, like . . . I don't know. You remember what we were saying about that kid who died?"

"The urban legend."

I stop and take the obit out of my pocket and hand it to him. "No legend," I say. "He's dead."

David looks surprised. He raises his eyebrows and says, "Hmmm." He hands me back the paper. "So . . . had you heard that and forgot, or maybe half heard it at school and it didn't sink in?"

"You mean, before I saw him on the computer?"

"Yeah."

I shake my head hard. "No. I had no idea. Nobody did. What Gary was saying the next day was a load of crap, but then it turns out that Bainer really was dead after all."

He lets out a low whistle. "The urban legend comes true."

We walk the rest of the way without talking. We go back on Main, me carrying a quart of milk and him with a six-pack of Long Trail Ale.

"So what did that have to do with the game?" he asks. "You said something about one of their players."

"This kid Scapes. He was always beating on Bainer. We showed him the obit and it shook him up. A lot."

"You too?"

"Yeah. I'm shook up. Last night when you were out, I saw Bainer on the computer screen again. Just a glimpse, but . . ."

David puts a hand on my shoulder and pats it. "Don't put much stock in that," he says. "When you get nervous and worried, you're bound to start seeing things. It's that power of suggestion I mentioned the other day. Guilt and fright and who knows what other psychological effects playing games with your perceptions."

After lunch (David insisted on making me a tuna-fish sandwich after the cereal), he tells me to get out and enjoy the day. "Forget about this dead kid for a while," he says. "Go shoot baskets in the park or something. The sunshine'll do you good."

But the sunshine doesn't last more than an hour, and I don't feel like shooting or hanging out with anybody, so I wander around on the streets for most of the afternoon.

Eventually I walk down a wobbly cobblestone alley between two brick buildings off Main. The buildings go far back, nearly a block, with apartments near the street but just dark empty windows and thick ivy climbing the walls toward the back. The end of the alley opens onto an old industrial area, lots of brick mill buildings either abandoned or converted to office space and shops—a shipping place with UPS and FedEx signs in the window, an accountant's office, the Classy Clippers hair salon. There are four very tall—five-story at least—silos crammed close to each other and looking ready to collapse, and several signs saying OFFICE SPACE FOR RENT or NO PARKING. It doesn't feel unsafe, just depressing. I can hear wheels screeching at the skateboard park, which is behind the auto parts store with the blue-painted cinder blocks. The blue paint is covered with graffiti that I can't quite decipher.

I take a seat at a wooden picnic table in the corner of a parking lot next to Papa's Tacos, a trailer that's only open on weekdays. A couple of blocks away I see kids on the swings behind the Catholic school.

I know why I ended up in this neighborhood today, but I'm reluctant to go farther. Still, I should take a look.

I get up and walk two blocks past college rentals—music blaring from most of them, guys sitting on the stoops with cans of beer and cigarettes, baseball caps on backward, some hibachis sizzling with hamburgers and sausages. TVs are tuned to college football games from Texas or Ohio; Cheshire Notch State doesn't have a team of its own.

Beyond those blocks, at the end of a dead-end street that's too desolate even for the students, is the house. It's tall and narrow, with gray asbestos siding peeling away and two of the windows covered in plywood. It's been empty ever since the Bainers moved out. There's a broken Dumpster in the yard overflowing with debris, and the lawn looks as if it hasn't been mowed or raked in more than a year.

Bainer used to ask me to come over, after school or on the weekend. I almost went once, back in fourth grade. Got this far and then turned back. Wouldn't risk being seen with him. And who knows what stupid stuff he would have pulled if I'd gone in.

I stare at the sad-looking house for a few minutes. No signs of life. On one side is an empty, run-down warehouse. On the other side is a junk-strewn yard and another dead house with a CONDEMNED sign on the door. Looks like a long time since anybody lived there. Three sneakers are hanging from a wire that connects the two houses.

There's a note on our kitchen table when I get back.

*Hey Jordan: Had to go home for something. Be
back early eve. Made the chicken, it's in the
frigerator. Hope you're feeling better. Have fun!*

Home? His home is in Boston, two hours away. If he had
time to cook the chicken, then he couldn't have gotten out of
here before three. It's quarter after five now.

Boston College is playing Georgia Tech, so I flop on the
couch to watch that. I'm way behind on sleep so I nod off in
about three seconds and stay there until the front door opens.

"Hey, buddy," David says.

"Hey. What'd you need in Boston?"

He points his thumb outside. "Picked up my other guitar.
These guys I met at the Shamrock, they're playing there to-
night and asked me to sit in. I figure it's an easy fifty bucks, but
I needed my ax."

So he'll be out tonight again, probably even later. I guess I
can watch another football game. Or two.

And go for another long walk if I have to.

CHAPTER SEVEN

It's all quiet in the house, but I can't bring myself to go up to the attic after dark. I keep glancing at the stairs and listening for that music, and it's got me scared stiff. The sky has cleared and the moon is just about full, so I put on a dark hooded sweatshirt and some black cotton gloves and go out. A strong wind is blowing in my face.

I pass the coffee shop and the Colonial Theater and turn at the bus station, walking through a parking lot and reaching the skateboard park. I scan the ramps but don't see anybody I know. Then I hear my name and see Scapes sitting on the curb twenty feet away in a filthy football jersey.

He juts his head in the direction I went earlier. "You go to the house?"

I give him a puzzled look. "Why?"

"I saw you heading that way this afternoon." He stands and puts one foot on his skateboard.

"How come you're not in there?" I ask, pointing at the chain-link fence, into the skating area, where a few older guys are on the ramps.

He frowns. "Still bummed out." He walks toward me, pushing his skateboard along with one foot. "Gary said you saw him. *After* he died. What's that all about?" He's stooping a bit, minimizing his size, seeming less intimidating. I can tell by his voice that he's spooked.

"I *think* I saw him." I give a huffy little laugh. "On this video. It sounds really stupid. It had to be less than twenty-four hours after he died, though. Just staring at me."

"What video?"

I roll my eyes. "My father was watching this concert from Japan or somewhere, and suddenly there's Bainer in the audience. But every time I went looking for it again, he wasn't there. And then it came on by itself and he was back."

"Did he say anything?"

"No. He just glared at me."

Scapes stands with his mouth hanging open, then looks around. He steps hard on the edge of his skateboard and it pops into the air and he catches it. "Ernie!" he yells to somebody inside the fence. "I'm leaving my board. Take it home."

He reaches over the fence and sets his board on the ground. Then he turns back to me. "Can you show me the video?"

I shrug. "He's usually not there."

"That's okay. Let's try, all right?"

So we walk back to my house. We don't say much. Halfway there he goes, "Gary says I killed him."

"He thinks we all did."

"Yeah, but he says I did the most."

Spike is on the steps, waiting to be let in. She rubs against my shin and meows.

"You want anything to drink?" I ask Scapes. "Seltzer? Sprite?"

"Nah. Clear liquids freak me out."

"They do?"

He blushes. "Yeah."

He follows me up the two flights of stairs. "You live in the attic?" he asks.

"I *sleep* in the attic. My computer's up here, too."

I know which of the many "Way Back into Love" videos it is now, so I find it quickly on the Freewheeler site.

"What is that?" Scapes asks as the woman starts speaking in Japanese.

"It's Asian," I say. "Don't ask how my father ever found this; who knows?"

"But Bainer's on it?"

I lower the volume. "Sometimes. I mean, he's not really *on* it, he just appears once in a while. Or he did."

The audience scan passes, but there's no sign of Bainer. "No," I say. "If he was gonna be there, it would've been by now."

Scapes leans closer to the screen and I can see the wispy, colorless beginnings of his mustache. "Run it again," he says. "Okay?"

I do, but it's the same. "He shows his face when he wants to, not because we're running the video. Last night it turned on by itself and there he was. Scared the piss out of me."

"I bet." He drums his fingers on his thigh, then rubs the corner of his mouth with his sleeve. He's looking around the attic, into the dark corners and up at the beams. "This is a cool space," he says.

"I like it. Or I did until Bainer started haunting me."

He shakes his head slowly. "Very weird. You think . . ."

"What?"

"You think a kid could die like that? From an accumulation of hits, even way after they happened?"

"Man, I don't know."

"I get banged around every day from boarding or playing football. It doesn't keep adding up. It heals."

"Yeah. Bainer didn't heal quick. One time he got this bruise in the middle of his forehead." The time I shoved him into the metal chairs. "It should have been gone in three days, but you could see it a month later." Near his brain.

Scapes is staring at the computer screen, which is frozen on the Freewheeler home page. He nods. "He bruised easy." He reaches to the screen and gently runs his fingers over it, like he's trying to see if it's hot or something. "You definitely saw him after he died? On here?"

I let out my breath in a short burst. "I don't even know anymore. The obit says he died on Tuesday. My parents left on Thursday morning, and it was the night before that, for sure. So yeah, he was dead. And his annoying face was right there on the screen, scowling at me."

He sits back abruptly. "Whoa. I can picture it."

"Tell me about it. I picture it every night. It wakes me up in my dreams."

He blinks a couple of times. "I got an idea," he says softly. "You have a flashlight?"

"Yeah."

"Get it. Maybe we can do something about this tonight."

The Bainer house is a lot scarier at night, lit only by the full moon, and only on one side. We look at it from the shadows of the old warehouse for several minutes, then Scapes points toward one of the boarded windows. "That one's loose," he whispers.

"You're going in?" I ask.

He gives me a half smile. "We are." He steps toward the

window and puts a hand on the board. It sways a bit. He gets his hand under it and pulls, and a nail makes an *aaaank*-y sound as it comes away from the frame. He pulls with both hands and the plywood falls with a dull thud as he jumps back.

"You ever been in there?" I whisper.

"Once. About five years ago."

That would have put us in second grade. Way before Bainer moved. "With him?"

He tightens his mouth. Then he clambers up and straddles the opening before ducking in. I follow. "I went to his birthday party," he says.

That's hard to believe. He does know the house, though, pointing out the living room and the kitchen as we wait for our eyes to adjust. I don't dare turn on the flashlight, to avoid attracting attention. "What are we doing here?" I ask.

"Like a séance. You know what that is?"

"Yeah." We keep our voices at a barely audible level.

"Maybe we can communicate with him."

The house is empty, at least down here, and it smells moldy and damp. One beam of moonlight is hitting the living room floor; the thin wooden boards are warped and dotted with paint stains. The oven door has been ripped off and is lying in a dusty alcove where the refrigerator must have been, and all of the windowsills are covered with dead flies.

"How are we going to do this?" I whisper.

He juts his chin toward the stairs. "His room was up there."

I slide my hand along the wooden banister as we slowly go up. The air tastes stale and the wallpaper is peeling.

He runs his fingers against the wall. "Bathroom," he says as he reaches a door on the left. He points his thumb across the hall. "That was his parents' room."

There are two other doors. He pulls the first one open to a stairway, obviously to the attic. The other door is already open. Bainer's room is right above the window we entered the house through.

We're facing away from the street, so I flick on the flashlight for a second and it lights up Bainer's mug: A school photograph on the wall. It looks like it's from third or fourth grade, secured with a thumbtack—no frame or anything. There's also a paperback Matt Christopher baseball novel on the floor and a pile of small, cheap toys—like from McDonald's Happy Meals—in the corner.

Scapes sits against the wall, facing the back of the house, and I sit across from him. We don't say anything for at least five minutes.

"Eerie," he finally whispers.

"Yeah."

He picks a plastic Batman from the pile of toys, Doc from the Seven Dwarfs, and a samurai, and stands them in a semicircle, facing him. He motions with his hand for me to get closer, and I scuffle over next to Doc. My heart is beating way harder than it should be.

From where Scapes is sitting he can reach Bainer's photo, and he gives it a gentle tug until the thumbtack comes loose. He sets the picture on the floor inside our circle. "Let me have that light," he says.

He sets it facedown on the floor, so there's only the slightest glow.

I try to swallow, but my mouth is dry. I suck some saliva off my tongue. "Now what?"

He taps a finger on the wooden floor a few times. "Bainer?" he whispers, looking up and around.

"Bainer . . . we're waiting," he says. "Come on. When you're ready."

I catch his eyes and he gives me a look that says something like, *Be patient.*

So we sit and wait. It's cold in here, but we're out of the wind. We sit very still, staring at the flashlight. Nothing moves.

After ten minutes the Batman tips over and makes a soft *plunk* on the floor. I keep staring for a minute, then glance over at Scapes. He lifts his eyebrows and opens one palm. "It's cheap plastic," he says, barely loud enough for me to hear. He gives me a nervous half smile. We leave Batman down.

Then there's a scrabbling sound above us, in the attic.

"Squirrels?" I say.

"Or rats."

The sound stops.

The glow is mesmerizing. Eventually I start feeling calmer and not cold at all.

The samurai is smaller than the other two figures, made of hard plastic with no moveable parts and a red painted-on mouth. It seems to take a tiny, almost imperceptible step forward, then steps back.

I wait two minutes. "You see that?" I whisper.

"What?"

"Did that sword guy move?"

I look over at Scapes. He wipes his mouth with his thumb. "I don't think so. . . . The light's funny; the moon and the wind and all. Makes things shimmer."

I nod slowly. I'm sure it was the light.

Ten more minutes pass. Twenty.

"Bainer?" he whispers again. "We're here."

There's no response, no more movement. Scapes picks up

the flashlight and shines it into the corners, where there are spiderwebs and cracked plaster. He tacks the picture onto the wall, just a few inches above the floor, and slides the toys beneath it.

He stands and whispers, with slightly more volume, "I'm sorry, Bainer. Rest in peace, man," and we make our way down the stairs.

We climb carefully out the window. He props the plywood against the side of the house, but we have no way of reattaching it. So we turn to go, and I hear a *thwack* as something with force hits the clapboards above our heads. Scapes shines the flashlight on the house and finds a fresh dent. He bends and picks up a rock that bounced near our feet, about the size of an egg.

"Let's get out of here," he says, and we hurry across the lawn back toward town.

We stand near Papa's Tacos for a few minutes. Scapes looks up at the sky. His voice is shaky and low. "In second grade—this is the only nice thing I ever remember Bainer doing—my father'd been yelling at me all morning and I was shook up. He was still drunk from the night before, like every morning, and he smacked me in the head and shoved me out the door in a T-shirt. It was twelve degrees outside. So I start running to school and Bainer comes up behind me. He says something stupid like he always does, but he takes off his coat and hands it to me. He's wearing a heavy sweater so he's okay, and I'm freezing my butt off so I take the coat."

Scapes glances toward the skate park. I know that the cops start coming by every half hour after ten to clear the place out, but the boarders go back within five minutes.

He lets out a sigh. "A few days later he asks me to come

to his birthday party. He did me that favor with the coat, so I go. It was me, his parents, and two kindergartners from down the street. Callas and some others hear about it and give me hell until I bust them all in the face, but after that I really started"—his voice seems to catch in his throat—"well, I picked on Bainer a lot more."

"To redeem yourself?"

He hacks up some stuff and spits. "Something like that," he says. "What a jerk."

I nod. "Yeah. He was."

"I'm not talking about him," he says. "I've been a jerk ever since that happened."

He shrugs and starts walking toward the skateboard park. I walk home. Lots to think about.

What happens when you die? Do you lie there in limbo while your bones decay, not getting free until every molecule in your body has turned to dust and you become part of the atmosphere again? Like a million years from now? Or do you float away from all of that the moment you die, entering some afterlife where everything's peaceful and light and all of your dead relatives are there to greet you?

And what if you've got scores to settle back on Earth? Some revenge to enact on anyone who might have helped hurry you along toward your death?

Our house is dark. Spike is lying on the couch, so I push her aside and turn on Comedy Central. Some woman is doing stand-up and I watch for a few minutes. I'm hungry, so I go out to the kitchen and fish around in the refrigerator, finding that chicken David cooked earlier. I yank off a leg and bite into it. Then I stop cold, hearing a familiar voice from the TV.

"So, I heard your father is working as a plumber's assistant."

59

I set the chicken leg on the counter and rush to the living room. It's still that woman, joking about sex. I stare at the TV. Was that a commercial I heard? I shut off the set and go back to the kitchen.

I take another bite of chicken. And then I hear Bainer again from the living room. "I need your help right away; I gotta leak in the sink."

The TV is on when I get there, but the screen is blank and the sound is nothing but fuzz. "Bainer," I say, really loud. "What are you doing?" I'm scared, but I'm mad. I hustle up to the attic and turn on my computer.

I run through that "Way Back into Love" video three times but don't see a trace of him. The moonlight is coming directly through my narrow window, making a long, thin patch of brightly glowing light on the floor. And in the light are three tiny silhouettes that look like a samurai and a dwarf and an action figure.

I'm losing it. I'm going crazy. I need to get out of here fast.

The Shamrock is much busier tonight, with crowds of college students standing in the alley smoking and talking on cell phones, and hundreds of others packed into the bar room. "Jumpin' Jack Flash" is making the walls vibrate. It feels like my whole brain is vibrating, too, but not from the music—from nerves and confusion.

I lean against a brick building across from the bar and listen. I figure the band will give it a rest at some point and David will come out for a smoke.

They go through "Dream On," "Midnight Rider," and "Born to Run," then some taped crap from Lady Gaga comes on, so I know the band's on a break. Ten minutes later David squeezes through the crowd with a woman with curly bleached hair.

I walk over.

"Jordan," David says. "What's going on?"

"Thought I'd check out the band."

"We sound good?"

"Yeah, from out here. You gonna be playing all night?"

"Another hour maybe. You okay?"

"Yeah," I say, though I'm not. "I guess."

The woman steps past me and lights a cigarette. "Hi, honey," she says in a raspy voice.

"Hi."

David gestures at her with an open palm. "This is Lydia. I knew her back in high school."

Lydia gives a short, high-pitched laugh. "He *ignored* me back in high school," she says. "What's your name again? Jordan? Listen, Jordan, this uncle of yours was something special back in the day. Now look at him"—she gives that awful cackling laugh again—"won't even buy me a drink."

"You didn't let me," he says with a grin. "Said that'd raise too many expectations."

She takes a long drag on her cigarette and studies him. "Okay," she says, blowing out the smoke. "You can buy me one. Or two."

David gives me a sheepish shrug. They start to go back inside. David says, "You're definitely okay, right?"

Lydia answers for me. "He's fine."

Yeah, thanks.

She rubs her cigarette out against the bricks, then tosses it into a puddle. "Right, honey?"

"Right," I say. No use saying anything else.

My hands are shaking as I reach Main Street. I'm seeing him everywhere now—the Internet, the television. But not outside my house. We sat in Bainer's own house for way over an hour and never saw a trace of him. Except maybe that rock that hit the house. And the samurai.

I walk back that way. I don't know why. Past the industrial area, through the college neighborhood.

There's Bainer's house, dark and empty.

My stomach is so tight I feel like I might throw up. The idea of going back to my house is terrifying. Things turn on, and I hear Bainer or see him. But he's never spoken to me; he just lets me know he's there. He's getting back at me in the best way he knows how. By scaring the living crap out of me.

I step across the lawn, halfway between the street and the window we climbed through earlier.

I was his only chance for a friend in this town, and I wouldn't do it. Wouldn't risk the shunning from everybody else. I was the only one who might have stepped up and thrown him a break, back when I could have used a friend, too. Instead, I turned against him. I hurt him and I pushed him away.

All those punches that Scapes and the others threw, all those insults and rejections and shoves. "Mine hurt worst, didn't they, Bainer?" I whisper as I take the final steps to the house and set my hand on the windowsill.

I taste bile in my throat and swallow hard. I hurt him physically and that helped finish him off. But I also hurt him deeper— right to his soul—and that sort of hurt doesn't ever go away.

Lorne Bainer was a total jerk.

But maybe I could have manned up and helped him.

I sit on our couch until almost three, wrapped in a blanket and shivering like crazy. David finally comes home, feels my forehead, and makes us hot chocolate.

"We rocked the place tonight," he says, pumping his shoulders as if he's still at the Shamrock, jamming on his guitar.

I stare straight ahead.

"You all right?" he asks. "Besides being cold, I mean?" He turns to the thermostat on the wall and amps it up.

"The TV turned on by itself," I say, wrapping both hands around the mug and breathing in the chocolaty steam.

He raises one eyebrow. "It was windy."

"The night before that my computer started up by itself, too."

He leans back in an armchair and smiles. "Old house. I bet there's a lot of faulty wiring in the walls. You get a storm or a big gust and it can cause power outages."

"The power didn't go off."

"Sometimes it's a split second that you barely notice. But then there's a surge when the power comes back, so electronic stuff will reboot by itself. Happens all the time."

Maybe so. But it's different when something reboots and you get Bainer's voice or a video that scares the piss out of you. That's no coincidence. That's a haunting.

Or insanity.

I'm not buying this power-surge theory. "I heard Bainer talking when the TV came on," I say. "Before that, too, but then I shut it off."

"Oh." David's tone sounds like he doesn't quite believe me but that he's pretty sure I believe it myself.

"I know that sounds ridiculous," I say. "It sounds ridiculous to me, too. But things keep happening."

He takes a deep breath and blows it out, and I can smell cigarettes and beer. "You're shook up, Jordan, so everything seems magnified. I admit that this is a weird situation, but everything that's happened—if you look at them one at a time—has an explanation, right?"

"One at a time, yeah. But this stuff keeps going down. I'm seeing his face or hearing his voice or having that creepy video show up on my computer. That's too many coincidences for me."

We sit quietly for a few minutes and I sip the hot chocolate.

"Think you can sleep?" he asks.

"Not up there."

He nods. "Stay here, then. Leave the kitchen light on. I'm really beat. I'll sleep in your parents' bed tonight."

"Okay." I set down the mug and shut my eyes. Having him in the house is better. I can probably sleep. A little.

CHAPTER EIGHT

Gary's phone call wakes me up around ten. "Get bagels?" he asks.

"Yeah. Gimme ten minutes."

David's rolling out dough for a pie crust when I get to the kitchen. I was so zonked I hadn't heard a thing.

"Sleep okay?" he asks.

"I guess so."

He gives me a little smirk. "No more disturbances?"

"Not lately. Is that apple?"

"Yep."

"I'm meeting Gary. But I'll be back for some of that."

I realize that I'm too hungry for bagels, so I get a small pizza instead. Gary buys two Milky Way bars and we walk toward his house.

"What'd you do last night?" he asks. He says it sort of accusingly, as if he already knows.

"Hung around."

"At the scene of the crime?"

"What are you talking about?"

"I saw you walking with Scapes."

"So?"

He shakes his head. "You're crazy."

"And what crime anyway? There were a *thousand* crimes committed on Bainer, if you want to look at it that way. And every one of us is guilty."

"I never hit him."

We've reached his house, so we don't say anything more until we're in his room with the door shut. The dog followed us in.

"What do mean, you never hit him?" I say. "You hit him. I hit him, too."

"That was nothing compared to what Scapes does to people. You're out of your mind hanging around with him, you know."

"I wasn't with him long."

"What'd you do?"

I let out my breath and peel a slice of pizza from the box. I take a bite and chew it slowly. "We snuck into Bainer's house."

"You went in there alone? With Scapes? Are you that stupid? Scapes is a murderer, Jordan. He could have left you there dead. They'd find your corpse in twenty years."

I take another bite. "Can I give Barney this crust?" I ask. The dog's been drooling on Gary's floor ever since I opened the box.

Gary looks at it while he chews his Milky Way, shifting his head from side to side. "Nah," he finally says. "I don't know what's in that crust. It might not be good for him."

Barney lets out a sigh and flops onto the floor.

"He's not a murderer," I say softly. "Nobody wanted Bainer dead. We were all just stupid, that's all. Stupid and gutless, but not murderers."

My dad called from Paris that afternoon and said they hadn't sealed any deals yet but they'll be home on Wednesday. David did most of the talking. I didn't say a word about my visits from Bainer.

We watched the Patriots game that afternoon and had scallops with rice for dinner, and a lot of pie. David's gone out "for an hour or so," but I don't expect him back anytime soon.

I'm totally exhausted from being up most of last night, and the couch isn't the most comfortable place I've ever slept. So I say the heck with it and climb the stairs to the attic.

Spike is on my bed. I scoot her off and lie down, but she jumps up again and stands on my back. She sleeps up here most nights, but I don't need the disturbance this time.

"Sorry, buddy," I say. "I need a solid sleep. School tomorrow." I lift her gently and set her on the stairs, then close my door to keep her out. It shuts with a *click* and I feel a chill in my gut.

I haven't slept in this bed the past two nights. I sink in and mold myself into the mattress and the pillow, stretching out and finally beginning to relax. It's quiet. I sleep.

My dream is of a window, the one into Bainer's house. I climb through and step to the floor, but there's nothing but a vast emptiness, and I fall and fall and then hit hard on my back. I press into the surface. It's my bed. I'm lying flat. I'm suddenly cold, but I'm sweating.

I prop myself up and glance around the attic. All's clear. I lie back down. I sleep again.

This time there's a floor when I pass through the window, and I shuffle across the dark, empty living room, up the staircase, and past those first two doors. I put my hand on the third doorknob, hesitate a second, and pull it open.

The attic stairs are lit softly by the moonlight. I hear a buzzing from the attic, steady and mechanical. It gets louder.

It wakes me up.

The buzzing is coming from my laptop, but the monitor is black, except for the screensaver. If I click the space bar, whatever is there will reveal itself. I'm not sure I want to see.

I wait a minute. The buzzing gets softer, then stops. I sit on the edge of the bed and reach for the space bar, holding my finger above it. I gulp, then press. The screen lights up. It's just my desktop: a handful of icons. There's an orange INSTANT MESSAGE lozenge flashing in the lower right. I hesitate, then click it. It says it's from LBAINER.

> Hello Jordan.

L. Bainer? Sure it is. Does Gary think I'm dumb enough to fall for that?

> **Jordan:** who r u?
> **LBainer:** Who do you think I am?
> **Jordan:** i know ur gary.

There's a long pause on the other end. He knows this is just too obvious.

> **LBainer:** I am who you think I am.
> **Jordan:** and i think ur gary.
> **LBainer:** No. I am who you REALLY
>   think I am.
> **Jordan:** yeah? prove it.

The computer shuts off. I hear Spike yowl outside my door and go scurrying down the stairs. Everything is dark, and then the computer beeps and whines and turns back on.

And I hear the opening notes of "Way Back into Love."

This is nuts. I scramble across the bed and reach for the doorknob. It's stuck.

I rattle it and pull it, but it won't turn at all. The video is playing loudly now; the grungy guy is singing in the shadows. Get me out of here.

I've never had this door closed before, never checked t see if it would lock. Why would it? I've never seen a key.

I dive across the bed and try to shut off the comput r, but it won't stop. The audience scan is coming up. I start pping keys and arrows, trying to get it to end.

And it does. The screen goes blank. The compu er shuts down with a *whisssssss*.

Power surges, right? I crawl to the window and l ok at the street. It's breezy out there, but nothing major. T e moon is still nearly full and it's casting a glow on the lawn. m panting as if I ran a hundred-meter dash.

The laptop starts up again, but this time the e's no music. I step to my door and try it again, but it's locke fast. The IM lozenge is flashing. I click it.

> **LBainer:** Hello, Jordan.
> **Jordan:** gary id come over thre ght
> now and pnch ur STUPID fac in but
> im lockd in the atttic. come o r here
> and letme out. the frnt door not
> locked
> **LBainer:** I wish I could help you, Jordan,
> but I'm afraid I can't.
> **Jordan:** i'l bust your head tomorow jerk
> if u dont get overhere now

LBainer: Sounds like you're scared, Jordan.
Jordan: Im not scared of anythng. and il' break ur nose if udon't stop this crap
LBainer: Buck-buck.
Jordan: yu r dead meat gary.
LBainer: Buck-buck-buck.

I go to my buddy list and click Gary's real IM name, but it says he's offline. I clear the screen, but another one pops up immediately.

LBainer: Say Jordan?
Jordan: what?
LBainer: Stop making that ugly face. It'll freeze like that forever.

I yank the power cord and throw it toward the wall. The laptop turns off. I stare at the screen and wipe my forehead with my hand. Then I try the door again, easier this time. It's still locked.

I pull my chair over to the window and watch for David to walk up the street. It takes at least an hour, but he shows.

I start yelling as loud as I can as soon as he enters the house. I hear him thumping up the stairs, calling, "What's the matter?"

"I'm locked in here. The door won't open."

"Hold on."

I hear the knob rattle, then turn. He pushes the door open and grins.

"It wouldn't open from this side," I say.

He grabs the interior knob and this time it does turn. "It was just stuck," he says. "This gadget's probably a hundred years old. Maybe more. You ever have trouble with it before?"

"I've never closed it."

The knobs are old round brass things. "They should be replaced," David says. "Leave the door open for now."

"Don't worry. I will. Light on, too."

"You're white as a ghost." He laughs. "Bad choice of words, huh? You gonna be okay?"

"Can't get much worse."

"Just yell if you need me."

"I will. If I can."

It's going to be another long night.

CHAPTER NINE

I sat like a zombie through all of my classes this morning, yawning and shaking my head to keep my eyes open. Scapes comes up to me at lunch and asks if anything more happened.

"Oh, nothing much," I say. "Got locked in my room. Heard Bainer talking on my television. The usual stuff when you start losing your mind."

He laughs nervously. "That was creepy in his house. It really felt like he was watching us."

I shrug. Things have been a lot eerier in my house than at Bainer's.

"Would you go back?" he asks.

"I don't know. I'd rather leave that place alone."

"Me too." He hesitates for a minute, then sits across from me. I've barely touched my disgusting corn dog, but I take a bite.

"His gums used to bleed all the time," Scapes says. "For no reason. Remember how he always had that phlegmy stuff between his teeth?"

The corn dog hasn't gotten too far down, and it suddenly comes racing back up. I spit it onto my tray and grimace as stomach acid burns my throat. I take a swig of grape drink and swish it around in my mouth.

Scapes looks at the floor and frowns. "I wish I knew what really happened to him, you know? Maybe we had nothing to do with it."

"Maybe."

"All I know is . . . all I know is I wouldn't do it again. Not any of it."

I dodge Gary after school and head out the back way, crossing the blacktop basketball court and turning up Marlboro Street. It's four blocks to my old elementary school. I walk as fast as I can. If anybody would know what happened to Bainer, it'd be the principal.

All of the students are gone and the janitor is pushing a wide mop along the hallway. I stick my head into the principal's office. "Mrs. Graham?"

"Yes?" I can tell that she recognizes me but is searching her brain for my name. "Jordan . . . How are you?" She steps out from behind her desk.

"I was wondering if you knew anything about Lorne Bainer."

She touches her lips with two fingers. "You mean, since he moved away?"

"Yeah. Since then."

She shakes her head slowly. "No, I haven't heard a thing. Were you hoping to contact him?"

No. He's taken care of that. "I was just wondering how he might be doing."

"Hmmm." She squints a little, sizing me up, probably wondering about my motivations. "Well, I know that they moved out of the country."

"Out of the *country?* Like to Canada or something?"

"Farther than that. His parents were from Germany, so they returned there."

"Oh. You haven't heard anything about him since?"

"Not at all. Sorry. I know you two were"—she squints a bit—"friendly?"

"Not exactly."

She leans against her desk and smiles at me.

I'm confused. "They didn't move to Pennsylvania? Or Japan?"

Her smile gets broader. "Oh no," she says. "The father was very . . . old-country, if you know what I mean. Very traditional. They were definitely going back to Europe."

"So as far as you know, he's okay?"

"As far as I know. Is anything wrong, Jordan?"

I shake my head. "No. I just was thinking about him lately. He wasn't treated so good around here."

She lets out her breath and stands straighter. "You're right about that. Lorne was . . . unusual. Some children used that against him."

"Yeah."

"It's nice that you're thinking of him."

I turn to go and mumble, "Thanks."

"Jordan."

"Yeah?"

"We've all been cruel to others at some point in our lives. Sometimes in a small way, sometimes more seriously. And sometimes, unfortunately, we never get the chance to atone for that."

74

I'm feeling squirmy now. She must know about that time I pushed him into the chairs.

"But we can learn from that, right?" she says. "We can do good turns for someone else and make the world a little better."

I swallow and try to say thanks again, but my throat is tight. So I just nod really hard and walk away toward home. I've got some research to do on the Internet.

* * *

miller funeral home davenport pa

I press *search* and the website pops up on my screen. The obituaries are listed by date, and the first page shows all of the ones from this month. Just as I was starting to suspect, there's no Bainer. I start clicking on them anyway.

The third one down shows *Brandon Matthews, Age 12.*

> Brandon Matthews of Davenport,
> Pennsylvania, died Tuesday, Nov. 12.
> He is survived by his parents, William
> and Natalie. He attended Lake Erie Middle
> School in Davenport and was a member
> of the city's First Presbyterian Church. He
> was born in Youngstown, Ohio, and attended
> Euclid Elementary School there before moving
> to Davenport.
>
> Funeral arrangements are by the Miller
> Funeral Home of Davenport.
>
> Memorial contributions can be made to
> the Leukemia Foundation at the University of
> Pittsburgh Medical Center.

It's the exact same obit with the names changed, and a cancer foundation instead of one for brain injuries. I click on the guest book and find the same sympathy wishes for Brandon Matthews: ". . . we're soothed that his lingering distress is over . . ."

I do another quick search just to make sure. There's no Western Pennsylvania University.

Gary. You bastard. Prepare for another bloody lip.

I've calmed down a little by the time I get to his house. We go up to his room and he shuts the door, even though nobody else is home but the dog.

Obviously, he did some cutting and pasting. I trusted his links and that made for a great hoax.

"But how did you get Bainer to show up on my computer?"

Gary bursts out laughing. "The links were easy. I just fished around online until I found the right obituary, copied it, and made my own document with Bainer's name in it. And it worked exactly like I wanted it to."

"What do you mean?" I'm getting angry again.

He smacks my arm. "This wasn't about you, man. When Scapes beat me up, I spent the next two weeks figuring out how I could get revenge. And when you said you'd seen Bainer on the Internet, it hit me: scare Scapes to death. Let him know that this crap he dishes out can be serious. Maybe even jail-time serious if it goes far enough."

He flops onto his bed and laughs again. "You were the perfect helper, even though you didn't know it. You were scared out of your wits, so Scapes bought everything we said. When I sent you those fake links to the obituary and the sympathy notices, it clinched it. I left you in limbo about it so I could turn the screws on Scapes even tighter."

I stare out the window. Barney is whimpering in the hall,

so I open the door and let him in. "So that's one part of it," I say. "The easy part."

"What do you mean?"

"How'd you get him on that video? How'd you get my computer to turn on by itself?"

Barney jumps onto the bed and Gary starts wrestling with him. "You really think you saw Bainer on some video?"

"You think I'm lying?"

"Okay," he says. "You *think* you saw him."

"I know I saw him."

"You didn't." He gently shoves Barney off the bed and sits up with his feet dangling. The bottoms of his white socks, just below the toes, say *Hanes* in red stitching. "Look," he says, "maybe some of these techno guys can do that—make images appear on somebody else's computer. But I don't know anything about stuff like that. And anyway, you said he showed up first on your father's screen. How would I have known that you were looking at that particular video, at that particular time, on your father's computer? How could anybody know that?"

"So what are you saying?"

"I'm saying that I had nothing to do with what you say you saw. I just picked up on what you told me the next day and took it from there, with that fake obituary and all. You were so convinced you'd seen Bainer's ugly mug on the screen, I figured I'd freak you out some and take Scapes down a notch in the process."

I think about each time I actually saw Bainer online, and I guess it was only three times. I also heard that music a bunch of times, but I'd been searching Freewheeler earlier those nights. . . .

"I did see him," I say firmly.

He shakes his head and smiles. "Like your uncle said, it was the power of suggestion. You thought you might have glimpsed him, and your imagination kicked in. Reading that obit made you all the more sure that you'd seen him. You saw a mirage, buddy."

I don't know what I saw, but it definitely wasn't my imagination.

He got me good, and he knows it. But this doesn't add up. Too many things happened that were out of Gary's control. I'm not done with this. And I have a very strong feeling Bainer isn't done yet either.

CHAPTER TEN

I do a "Lorne Bainer" search on the Internet and find nothing—no sign that he's dead, no sign that he's alive—then I study that stupid "Way Back into Love" video a couple of times. Uncle David's been downstairs watching reruns of *Family Guy* and *The Simpsons* all evening.

When I hear him turn on the shower around nine thirty, I put on my sweatshirt and gloves and slip out of the house. If he even notices that I'm gone, he'll figure that I'm over at Gary's.

Our street is very dark and heavily tree-lined, so I'm out of sight of the house in seconds. I test the flashlight quickly after turning the corner. It works fine.

I take my time walking the back streets, but I'm pumped up. I'm scared, yeah, but I'm also excited. Bainer is out there somewhere—cyberspace or afterlife or maybe just over in Europe. But he's had his eye on me all week, and I've had enough of it.

This is my city; I've never lived anywhere else. I'm not going to be driven out of town—or out of my mind—by some annoying kid who hasn't been around for eighteen months. (Not in the flesh anyway.)

I cross Main before I get downtown and cut through the edge of the college. There are lots of people over by the student center and walking the paths, and an Aerosmith song is blasting from an open dorm window. I stay in the shadows, scuffing through leaves and acorns.

I pass the rows of off-campus houses and head for Bainer's. There are sounds in the distance—students talking on a porch, an airplane overhead, traffic on Main Street—but I feel cut off from the town back here, a good block away from any signs of life. The air is clear and cold.

I walk slowly across the lawn, and the wind lifts a few leaves into the air. Something scurries through the brush over by the empty warehouse—a cat or a possum maybe.

I put a hand inside the windowsill, place my foot against the stone foundation, and haul myself up. I step to the floor as gently as I can, trying to avoid making any sound.

Then I breathe. My heart is racing. I wait for my eyes to adjust and my nerves to steady. I slide my back down the wall and take a seat.

There's nothing to see down here, but I sit for ten minutes, letting the house get used to me, allowing the energy to settle.

I don't even need the flashlight, but I take it with me as I cross the living room and tiptoe up the stairs. What will I do up here? Try to talk to Bainer? Just sit and wait until something happens?

I catch my breath sharply—the attic door is open. I know we didn't leave it like that.

I edge up to it and flick on the flashlight, since the hallway going up is pitch dark.

"God!" I jump back.

The tiny samurai is on the first step, facing me. Two steps

farther up is the Batman, its right arm raised as if it's pointing to the attic. Doc is waiting on the next-to-last step.

Somebody's been here, I guess.

I poke my head into Bainer's room, but it's empty, so I take a deep breath and slowly climb the attic stairs.

The attic is a big open space—no partitions or rooms, just bare floorboards and exposed beams overhead.

Something flutters down from the ceiling and I jump. A bat? No. I shine the flashlight and see that photo of Bainer, the one that was tacked to the wall in his bedroom the other night. I can't bring myself to reach down and pick it up.

The light catches a cardboard box in the corner, covered with dust. I step toward it and swallow.

The box is square, about two feet high and wide. *LORNE THINGS* is scrawled on the flap in black marker.

I unfold the top, holding the flashlight in my armpit. Then I pull out a handful of papers and set them on the floor.

His report card from fifth grade, all Bs and Cs. A couple of school photos. A sealed envelope with *Mr. and Mrs. Bainer* handwritten on the outside.

I hesitate, then carefully tear open the envelope. Inside is a note from our fifth-grade teacher.

Mrs. Graham has informed me that you've decided not to take advantage of the counseling that was offered to Lorne. I urge you to reconsider. Lorne is a bright boy, but he has extreme difficulty fitting in with his classmates. Some sessions with a psychologist could do him a world of good and help him adjust

Sincerely,
Gloria Munson

The next paper is a simple list in Bainer's handwriting: *Invite to birthday*. There are four of us on the list. Me and three people I don't even recognize. Maybe from his church or something.

I never got that invitation. Probably nobody did.

Why did they leave all this stuff behind? Maybe it was too painful to take.

And here's the script he wrote for that comedy routine that never happened. It has some reasonably funny jokes.

> *Me: How come your father didn't come to the show?*
>
> *Jordan: He went hunting bear.*
>
> *Me: Well, he should have put on some clothing.*

Another piece of paper. It looks something like a form for a prescription, with *Douglas Schuter, MD*, at the top and the doctor's address, dated just before the Bainers left the country.

I scan it: Cheshire Medical Center . . . Lorne Bainer, male, 11 years . . .

And then I hear my name. Clear. From the second floor. It's not a voice I recognize. Not Scapes or Gary or any guy. It sounds like the tone of a bell, or a song. Just my name: "Jordan."

I freeze and slip the paper into my pocket.

I've heard no footsteps. No one entering the house or climbing the stairs. I listen hard, but there's nothing.

But there must be something. Something called my name. My breath is short and cold and the back of my neck is sweaty.

An attic step creaks ever so slightly. I back against the wall, crouching behind the box.

Those stairs are the only way out of this attic.

Fifteen minutes have passed, but there hasn't been another sound or any movement. I'm cold. Petrified. I can't bring myself to move.

The voice sounded pure, like it was floating in the air and detached from any person. It went right through me; it feels like it's still vibrating in my chest.

Another attic step creaks. This one sounds closer. I grip the flashlight tighter; it's my only weapon.

There are four small windows up here, but it's a three-story drop straight to the ground. Broken legs, at least. I'll take my chances for now.

Another creak, and then I hear the plastic toys clunking down the stairs. I put one hand on the cardboard box and squeeze, just staring at the opening in the floor where whatever it is would emerge.

The shadows seem to shift in the attic, as if the faintest glimmer of light has moved in. It's everywhere at first, and then localized in the corner directly across from me. It's like that almost-imperceptible glow from the facedown flashlight when me and Scapes were in Bainer's room. Too soft for me to make out any shape—just a presence.

I swallow hard and turn on my light, aiming it toward the glow. It's grayish and my size and it moves slowly, like an animal—wary and controlled. I think I see a head, two arms.

I'm across the attic and onto the stairs in less than a second, taking them three at a time and pivoting as I reach the bottom. My feet slide out from under me—Batman and Doc cracking from my weight and shooting away from me as I go down hard, feeling intense pain in my forearm.

I push up and hear "Jordan" in that same eerie voice from

upstairs. My face is dripping with sweat and tears as I hobble down the next flight of steps.

I reach the front door and yank it open with my good arm and stumble onto the lawn.

"Come back and play, Jordan," I hear. "I only want to be your friend."

I run a few steps, but my arm hurts too much. I pull it against my body and wince. "I wish I could," I say, turning toward the house. "I wish I'd tried back then."

I see a flicker of light in Bainer's room, then the shadow of a person on the wall.

The house goes dark, and I step away. But then I hear footsteps or something behind me, and I shiver and turn and see a swirl of dried leaves scooting toward the back of the yard.

And despite the pain and my fear, I walk toward the swirl until it stops and seems to hover. The leaves slowly fall to the ground.

"Go back, Bainer," I whisper. "Wherever you've been, go back there and start over. There's nothing I can do for you here."

The leaves rustle up again, then settle. I stare at the pile for a couple of minutes, then back away and walk home.

Gary comes to our house late the next afternoon, bringing me my history book and a homework assignment. He signs the cast on my arm—*Happy Ghostbusting!*—and asks if I'll be able to play in Saturday's basketball game.

"Are you nuts?" I ask. "I'm out for the season."

"Big loss."

Uncle David managed to reach my parents this morning, but he told them not to pay for an earlier flight home. "He's tough," I heard him say. "It's just a hairline fracture."

He tripped up a bit trying to explain how it happened, but then again, he didn't have much to go on. My story was that I went for a jog to get in better shape for basketball. Fell on the bumpy sidewalk. That's what I told Gary, too.

"What really happened?" Gary asks me now.

"I slid down those attic stairs. Trying to get out of there as fast as humanly possible."

"Because of an inhuman presence?" He laughs.

I don't laugh back. "Something like that." I shake my head. I'm not ready to talk about it with him or anybody else. But I do think it's over.

Maybe Bainer died from all those beatings, and maybe he didn't. Maybe he's been haunting me for the past five days, and maybe he hasn't. I found that paper from the box in his attic in my pocket this morning. It said Lorne was scheduled to start chemotherapy right before they moved. That's how they treat cancer. Maybe they went back to Europe so he could get better treatment. Or maybe they just ignored it, like that letter from Mrs. Munson.

Like Uncle David said about these urban legends: there's always a kernel of truth behind them. You poke around, looking for that truth, but you usually come up empty. Instead, you find half-truths and fiction, and the reality disappears into myth.

But the myths don't come from nowhere. Somewhere in the past some creepy event really did happen to start the story. This one started here. This week. And I lived through it.

The legend of Lorne Bainer has a lot more truth to it than fiction.

THE HORSES OF BRICKYARD POND

Tragedy. A century ago, a team of horses drowned in a flooded

brickyard, snuffed out at the height of their power. But sometimes,

on dark, rainy nights, they summon all their vigor and run free.

Danny closed his bedroom door tight and walked to the bathroom. He leaned over the sink and pried up his left nostril, examining it in the mirror. It looked dry in there. Empty. No more blood.

"Danny!" Claudine called from the bottom of the stairs. "The pasta's ready! Mom says to get down here. Now!"

He pulled the note from his pocket and considered throwing it away. But then he walked down to the kitchen.

"Here's a note from the nurse," he said, handing the envelope to his father. "It's no big deal."

"Did you get hurt at school?" Mom asked, setting down a slotted spoon that she'd been using to stir the pasta.

"I had a bloody nose," Danny said. "It was nothing. She said she had to send a note anyway."

Dad unfolded the paper and read it. "What's this mean?" he asked, squinting. "'Nosebleed. Likely due to digital manipulation.'"

"It means he was picking his nose!" said Claudine.

"Lay off," Mom said. "Did you get any on your shirt, Danny?"

"Snot?"

"*Blood.* Snot washes out, but blood stains."

"Maybe a little," Danny replied.

"Well, get the shirt. I'll spray some pre-wash on it."

Danny walked back up the stairs.

"Pick me a winner!" called Claudine.

"Bite me," Danny mumbled.

It was a good shirt. Light blue with a collar and buttons all the way down. The kind you'd wear if you worked at a convenience store or a quick-lube car place. Danny held it up. There were three drops of blood near the chest pocket. Two were smaller than a kernel of corn. The third was the size of a nickel. They were a dark, rusty red.

"That's bone-dry," Mom said, poking at the spots with her thumb. "How long ago was this nosebleed?"

"I think that one was around noon."

"You had more than one?"

Danny frowned and sat down. He scooped a heap of pasta onto his plate. "It was bleeding when I got to school this morning. I stopped it up with toilet paper. Then it bled some more at lunch. Just a few drops, but I didn't feel it coming, so it landed on my shirt."

"That's 'cause you dug out the boogers," Claudine said. "They were holding back the blood."

"Mind your own business," Danny said.

Dad cleared his throat. "This isn't an appropriate subject for the dinner table."

"Better watch what's *under* the table," Claudine said. "That's where he wipes it."

"Enough," Mom said. "Is this a problem, Danny? Have you been having a lot of nosebleeds?"

"Just those two."

"Then let's forget about it. No worries."

"Fine with me."

"But be careful when you pick," Mom said. "Sometimes it's better just to leave it in there."

Dad set his fork down hard. "Can we please move on to something else?"

"It's perfectly natural, Byron."

"Yes, dear, I know that full well. But there are a lot of natural things we don't talk about over spaghetti."

Claudine laughed. "Dad's squeamish."

"He must have looked at your face," Danny said.

Claudine put her hand to her heart and gasped. "*Biting* sarcasm, Danny. Such a clever wit."

"Cleverer than you."

"More clever."

"Like I said."

Dad set his fork down even harder. "How old are you two? Will this go on forever? Most brothers and sisters get along, you know. Maybe not when they're children, but you two are teenagers!"

"She is," Danny said, pointing at Claudine, who would turn fourteen in a few weeks. She didn't *look* fourteen, still holding on to baby fat and her straight, unfashionable hair. Danny wouldn't be thirteen until summer, and he didn't look his age either—short and freckly and bony.

"He's so disgusting," Claudine said. "He never washes his feet."

"How would you know?" Danny asked.

"You *told* me. And this nose-picking thing . . . Have you guys ever looked at the side of the couch? It's like a green wall of snot."

Mom shivered and looked at Danny. "Is that true?"

Danny shook his head.

"Take a look after dinner, Mom," Claudine said. "Not you, Dad. I know it would upset you terribly. Especially after this lovely spaghetti."

"What's wrong with the spaghetti?" Mom asked with surprise.

"Nothing, Mom," Claudine moaned. "I always look forward to it on the fourth night in a row."

"Danny," Mom said, "you don't really wipe snot on the side of the couch, do you?"

"No."

"Yes, he *does*," Claudine said. "Every time he watches TV. Go take a look."

"I do not!"

"Enough!" Dad said. He picked up his fork and set it down much harder than the last time. "Not another word about nose picking, please. . . . And the word is *mucus*."

Claudine looked at her plate and rolled her eyes. "He's so immature," she muttered.

"*You're* immature," Danny said.

They ate in silence for a few minutes. Mom cleared her throat. Dad carefully picked a scrap of green matter from the tomato sauce on his plate and set it on his napkin.

"I hope that's not what I think it is," Claudine said.

"I don't care for olives in my spaghetti sauce," Dad said, raising his graying eyebrows at Mom. "That's a well-established fact."

"Maybe it's not an olive," Claudine said. "Maybe Danny wiped something into the pot."

"Real funny," Danny said. "Ha-ha."

"You know, you can give yourself a brain infection by sticking your filthy fingers up your nose," Claudine said.

"Can*not.*"

"Yes, you can. They told us about it in health class. There's only a very thin layer of skin between the back of your nostril and the brain cavity. When you make it bleed, you're exposing your brain to all kinds of bacteria." She sat back and gave Danny a smug look.

"At least I *have* a brain," he said.

"Oh, and I don't?"

"Not as far as I can tell."

Claudine made her voice very high and whiny as she imitated her brother. " 'Not as far as I can tell.' "

Dad pushed his chair back and set both hands on the table. He spoke evenly but with some heat. "I've had just about enough of this."

"Save it for your students, Byron," said Mom, who was much younger than her husband and had once actually been his student. "We don't need another speech."

"Is it really too much to ask to have one peaceful meal a day in this house?" Dad said. "I should run a tape recorder. We can play it back and you children could hear just how petty and *ridiculous* you sound. Really. Petty and ridiculous."

Danny looked across at Claudine. He could tell that she was holding back a smile. He bit on his lip to stop from laughing. But he laughed anyway, and so did Claudine.

"Nice lecture, Byron," Mom said. "Now sit still and eat your dinner."

Danny grabbed the pepper mill and ground it onto his pasta. Claudine took a sip of water. Dad wound some spaghetti onto his fork and chewed carefully with his mouth tightly closed.

"And by the way," Mom said, "I didn't put any olives in the sauce."

                              *   *   *

Danny washed his feet twice that evening, once at the beginning of his shower and once at the end. Then he sat at his desk
near his bedroom window, leaving the light off.

The moon was up and it was shining brightly on Brickyard Pond, about fifty yards away. The pond was on the campus of Cheshire Notch State College, and it began at the edge
of Danny's backyard. The site of the pond really had been a
brickyard at one time, more than a hundred years ago. It had
produced the bricks for many of the college's buildings before
being flooded.

The legend was that one day a worker dug into the clay
and sliced into an underground aquifer. Water burst into the
brickyard so quickly that the man barely escaped. A team of
horses got bogged in the mud and drowned. It's said that on
dark and rainy nights, you can sometimes hear the horses trying to gallop to safety.

Danny thought quickly of Janelle, the girl who sat one row
in front of him and one seat over in class. Her dark, shiny hair
was pulled into a tight braided ponytail, like a horse's mane.
She was always nice to him. She was nice to everybody.

He turned on his light, picked up a comic book, and
flopped onto his bed.

He heard the sound of knuckles rapping on his bedroom
door. Only one person rapped like that.

"It's open, Dad."

The door swung smoothly. Dad cleared his throat. "I have
a few thoughts I'd like to share with you," he said. He was
holding an old book. It had no jacket, and the hard-cloth cover
had faded to a ragged pink.

With his pointing finger, Danny pushed his glasses back up

on his nose and swung his legs off the bed, sitting on the edge. "I'm all ears."

Dad took a breath and let it out slowly. His hair was short and mostly gray. He sat on the edge of the bed, too, but barely, as if he might jump up at any second. He scratched at his carefully trimmed beard and sighed. "I spoke to your sister, too, so don't assume I'm only coming down on you."

"I won't."

"You know . . ." Dad spread his hand and studied the palm. "I didn't have the privilege of siblings. My parents were older, and I came along relatively late in their life, as you did in mine. Your mother and I, well . . . not to put too fine a point on it, but you were in some ways a gift we created for your sister. And *she* was a gift that was waiting for you to arrive."

"Happy birthday," Danny mumbled.

Dad raised his palm. "I hope—I *sincerely* hope—that you two will come to appreciate each other. And soon. This constant bickering has gone on far too long."

"It's no big deal," Danny said.

"Nonetheless," Dad said. He opened the book. "This poem is called 'To My Sister,' and I'd like you to listen to a portion of it."

"Oh, God."

"Just a few lines."

"Is this Wordsworth again?"

"Indeed."

Danny shut his eyes and dropped back on his pillow. "Lay it on me."

Dad cleared his throat again. "This was written more than two centuries ago, but it's terribly relevant today," he said. "Especially in this household." He began reading from the middle of the poem.

> My sister! ('tis a wish of mine)
> Now that our morning meal is done,
> Make haste, your morning task resign;
> Come forth and feel the sun.

Danny rolled onto his face. *This is agony,* he thought. *Make him stop!*

> Then come, my Sister! Come, I pray,
> With speed put on your woodland dress;
> And bring no book: for this one day
> We'll give to idleness.

Dad stopped reading. Danny opened his eyes. "Is it over?" he asked.

"That's the end of the poem, yes."

"Praise the Lord."

"Danny!"

"Sorry, Dad. Couldn't they just speak *English* back then?"

"The finest," Dad said. "Did you grasp what the poet was saying?"

Danny shrugged. "Sure."

"He appreciated his sister, didn't he?"

"Yes, Dad. I *get* it."

"Good," Dad said, carefully closing the book. "Good. All I ask is that you reflect on those lines a bit."

"Will do."

Dad stepped away.

"What did you read to Claudine?"

Dad stood still for a moment, deep in thought. "'There Was a Boy,' by the same poet," he finally said. "It's about a young lad, of course. Same age as you."

Dad held the book to his lips. When he spoke again, his voice was very soft. "I read her the entire poem. . . . I'll share the last stanza with you."

Danny propped himself on his elbows to listen. He heard the toilet flush across the hall.

> And, through that church-yard when my way has led
> On summer-evenings, I believe, that there
> A long half-hour together I have stood
> Mute—looking at the grave in which he lies!

"The kid died?"

Dad nodded.

"Great. I'll sleep real well tonight."

"It has a broader meaning than death."

"Okay. Tell Claudine to leave her gifts of gratitude outside my door. We'll offer our mutual appreciation in the morning."

"Just think it over, Danny," Dad said. "A sister is a wonderful thing." He hesitated in the doorway for a moment. Danny didn't look up.

"This is a fragile volume," Dad said, "from 1898. You'd find the same poem in some of the later editions in my office."

"Oh."

"It's called 'There Was a Boy.'"

"Right, Dad. I got it."

Danny woke early and walked over to the pond. He could fish for a half hour before school. The pond was only the size of three football fields, but he'd caught a few small bass last summer.

This was the quietest and most remote part of the campus, with dirt paths and maple trees. The college's performing arts center was on the other side of the pond, but then there was a border of woods and no other nearby buildings.

The morning was cold—probably below freezing—and a chill mist was rising from the water. Red and yellow leaves were floating near the banks. Nothing was biting today, not even sunnies, but being alone in what passed for wilderness was one of Danny's favorite things to do.

He didn't quite fit in with other kids, and he knew it. He'd joke around with them at school, and once in a while he'd get in a game of basketball or touch football on a weekend. But he didn't have a best friend or a group that he hung out with. Lonely? Sometimes. Maybe even often. But never out here by the pond.

He gave up on fishing after twenty minutes and walked to the arts center to check the posters. Sometimes there were events worth seeing.

The upcoming film schedule included *Night of the Living Dead* on Halloween. There was also a poster for the town's annual Pumpkin Fest, which was a huge deal in downtown Cheshire Notch. That was only two days away.

And then Danny saw his father gazing at him from a black-and-white notice:

POETRY READING AND BOOK SIGNING

Wordsworth scholar Byron Morgan, PhD, adjunct professor in the Cheshire Notch State College Department of English, will read from his new collection of poetry—*Monadnock Reflections*—at 7 p.m., Saturday, October 28, in the Brickyard Arts Center Auditorium. Admission is free.

Danny figured he'd have to be there, even though he'd heard every poem his father had written about Mount Monadnock a hundred times. Over the years, a few of the poems had been published locally, in the *Daily Sentinel,* the *Monadnock Shopper,* and the *Cheshire Notch State College Literary Review.* The rest would be appearing in print for the first time.

Danny could see the mountain from here.

The town of Cheshire Notch, New Hampshire, sits in a valley and is mostly flat, so Mount Monadnock appears particularly regal as it overlooks the town. It has the classic Alpine shape, with a sharp peak, and its treeless, granite summit majestically reflects the sun's rays.

Danny picked up a flat stone and skimmed it over the pond. It took one big skip and two shorter ones before sinking below the surface. The rings spread out and disappeared.

He and Claudine were the fourth generation of Morgans to live in the white clapboard house near the pond. Their father's grandfather had built the house not long after the brickyard flooded over. The family history was sketchy prior to that.

Danny wanted to see those ghost horses some night. He'd heard that you could feel their fear as they struggled to escape the flood, see their flared nostrils and hear their desperate whinnying. And on certain nights they *would* break free, leaping from the water and racing circles around the path.

But he'd never seen them. And he'd spent lots of nights by his window, just looking out. Twice he thought he'd heard distant hoofbeats, but he was never quite sure.

Four members of the college cross-country team jogged past as Danny headed for home, shuffling through the fallen leaves.

"It's late," Mom said as he entered the kitchen. "Pour yourself some cereal and wash your hands. Claudine already left."

"She always leaves too early."

"Well, she likes to see her friends. Now get moving."

Danny ran up the stairs and washed off the bait smell. *What friends?* he thought. Claudine wasn't any more popular than he was.

He brushed his teeth and gathered his stuff for school, then leaned on the windowsill and gazed out at the pond. He let out his breath in a long, steady burst that fogged the window, then stepped across the hall to his father's office.

"There Was a Boy" was easy to find. It was also easier to read than most of the poetry Danny's father had imposed on him over the years. He scanned the lines:

> *At evening, when the earliest stars began*
> *To move along the edges of the hills,*
> *Rising or setting, would he stand alone,*
> *Beneath the trees, or by the glimmering lake*

"Danny!" called his mother. "You need to *go!*"

He closed the book and carefully put it on the shelf. Then he grabbed his backpack and ran down the stairs. Mom handed him a peanut butter sandwich and told him he'd better keep running.

Danny heard a distinct *pssshhhhttt* sound as he closed his locker. Luke was giggling. He was in Danny's seventh-grade class and was seven inches taller and a whole lot stronger. It'd been Luke's elbow that had caused that first nosebleed at school the day before. Luke said he didn't mean it, but it was hard to see how. Danny had leaned over to pick up a pen that had dropped off his desk. When he came back up, Luke's elbow happened to be in the aisle. When Danny cleaned his nose out with his finger a couple of hours later, it started bleeding again.

Luke caught Danny's eye and held up the bottle of soda, then started chugging it down. His friend Carter was doing the same.

"Ahhh," Luke said, wiping his mouth. "Nothing like warm Coke."

"Gross," Danny said. "Why didn't you just get a cold one?"

"You'll see," Luke said. "Warm is perfect."

Danny followed Luke and Carter into the classroom. They had a few minutes to kill. Danny sat down and looked at Janelle. She was studying a sheet of paper, but she turned to look after a minute. She smiled at Danny. "How was your lunch?"

"Terrible," he said. "Glop with tater tots. You?"

"I brought my own. But I like glop. Was it brown or gray?"

"A little of both. And some yellow."

"Mmmm. Yellowish glop."

"There's probably some left over," Danny said with a grin. "I could fish it out of the Dumpster for you after school if you want."

"That would be great."

Danny felt someone leaning toward him, and suddenly a very wet *buuuuurp* exploded inches from his ear. It smelled like sausages and warm Coke.

"That's disgusting!" Danny said.

Janelle was laughing, so Danny tried to, too. Luke and Carter were high-fiving each other.

They burped and farted several times over the next half hour. Mr. Barnes asked Luke if he needed to see the nurse or use the restroom, but he didn't say it with much sympathy.

Most of the kids in the class were very amused. Danny

might have been, too, if he hadn't received a wet earful of it before class.

On Saturday morning there was a cold, light mist, but the sun was supposed to break through in time for the Pumpkin Fest. Danny liked going downtown early to watch them set up the scaffolding. There would be nearly thirty thousand carved pumpkins on those scaffolds, stacked as high as forty feet in the air. At night they'd all be lit, creating a spectacle that was hard to put into words. It was bright and orange and spirited.

Every school kid in town, every Scout troop, every youth group had spent the week carving jack-o'-lantern faces. Danny's contribution had a big wide grin and two lopsided teeth. It had taken ten minutes to cut during homeroom. He'd been told it would be on Main Street near the Colonial Theater with the other middle-schoolers' pumpkins.

"I suppose your mother will drag me into town this afternoon," Dad said as Danny was getting ready to leave. "Maybe we'll see you there."

Dad didn't care for the crowds. The Pumpkin Fest attracted seventy-five thousand visitors to town for the day, from all over New Hampshire and Vermont and Massachusetts, including a few busloads from Boston.

Danny's favorite part of the whole thing—besides the jack-o'-lanterns—was the food. The ambulance corps, church groups, Little League teams, Special Olympics—those and dozens of other organizations sold doughnuts, pizzas, pierogies, cider, and countless other food items, earning most of their budget for the year on this single day.

"Dress in layers," Mom said. "You can always shed some things if it warms up."

Layer one: T-shirt, Danny thought. *Layer two: sweatshirt.*

"Mom! He's trying to leave without a jacket," Claudine said as Danny opened the back door.

"Danny," Mom said. "They say it might be stormy later."

He pulled a Red Sox jacket from a hook. "Thanks, jerk," he said to Claudine.

"You're *so* welcome."

"Don't you two forget about your father's poetry reading tonight," Mom said.

"Mom," Danny complained, "that's when they start lighting the pumpkins."

"They'll be lit until midnight. You can miss a little of it."

Claudine scowled. "That's when, like, twenty of my friends are meeting to hang out," she said. "Can we just stay a few minutes?"

"No," Mom said. "The entire poetry reading will be less than an hour. You need to be there."

Claudine walked out of the room, muttering, "Why do I have to be the daughter of a famous poet?"

Danny put on the Red Sox jacket and left the house. *Right, Claudine,* he thought. *Dad's famous and you have twenty friends. And Santa Claus is married to the Easter Bunny.*

Main Street was closed to traffic for the day, starting at the roundabout, so Danny walked down the center of the road past huge brick houses and the post office and St. Joseph's Church. Dozens of giant pumpkins were set up on the center median here, some of them as tall as he was. The food vendors started a block later, with tents and booths and grills lining both sides of the wide street.

Danny could smell chicken roasting. There would be at

least two rock or jazz performances going on at any time, under tents or on temporary stages around town.

A lot of people were already walking. By noon it would be so crowded that you could barely move.

Danny found his jack-o'-lantern on the lowest row of a five-platform scaffold. He looked around, then lifted the pumpkin and placed it two rows higher, close to eye level and next to Janelle's, which she'd carved with much greater delicacy and skill.

"Beauty and the beast?" asked a familiar voice.

Danny turned to see Luke pointing at the two pumpkins and laughing. Luke was wearing a sleeveless T-shirt and shorts; didn't seem like any parents told *him* what to wear.

Carter was standing with him. Carter never said much; he just hung close to Luke all the time.

"As if you've got a chance with Janelle," Luke said. "Those two pumpkins are closer than you'll ever get to her."

"What are you talking about?" Danny asked.

"Like we don't know you have a crush on her?" Luke said. "Everybody sees you staring at her in class."

"I do not."

"You do, too."

"I do not!"

"You do it every day."

"So what if I do?"

Luke turned Danny's pumpkin and pushed it slightly, so its mouth was up against Janelle's pumpkin. "Look. Your pumpkins are making out. That's as close as you'll ever get."

"Cut it out," Danny said. He readjusted the pumpkins.

"We're just kidding around, Danny Boy," Luke said. "Dream about her all you want."

Luke and Carter walked away, laughing.

"Jerks," Danny said. He said it out loud, but not nearly loud enough for anyone else to hear.

By noon Danny had eaten a container of French fries from the fire department, a pulled-pork sandwich made by a church choir, and a slice of pumpkin pie from a Girl Scout troop. He had his eye on some chicken fingers and kettle corn.

A teenage grunge-rock band had started playing in the parking lot in front of Cheshire Tire, so he made his way through the crowd to listen. He squeezed between two people in motorcycle jackets and found himself standing next to the last person he'd hoped to see: his sister, Claudine.

Claudine rolled her eyes and took two sideways steps away. Someone else moved into the gap.

Janelle.

She was his height, and she seemed to glow with fitness and confidence. She was gyrating her shoulders in rhythm to the music, which must have been hard because it didn't seem to Danny that there *was* any rhythm.

Janelle was the first girl Danny had ever thought was beautiful. When he caught her eye, she seemed to brighten, and she made a motion with her hand that looked like a duck's beak closing.

Danny waved, too, a sweeping, open-palmed gesture. He lifted one shoulder and dropped the other in imitation of her dance, then immediately stopped trying to be cool.

He could see Claudine looking over in disgust. Janelle turned to her and smiled, and Claudine sunk back into the crowd and disappeared.

"Your sister doesn't like you much, huh?" Janelle asked while the musicians broke between songs.

"I don't like her much either."

"Why not?"

"She's . . ." Danny hesitated. His father had told him—repeatedly—that speaking ill of others would not endear you to anyone else. "She's at an awkward age," he said, a phrase his father constantly used when referring to Danny.

Janelle gave a half smile. She was the best-liked kid in class. "What age *isn't* awkward?"

The band started up again, intentionally off-key and sullen. Janelle leaned toward Danny and jutted her chin toward the drummer. "That's my brother," she said.

"You get along?"

Janelle nodded vigorously. "Really well. But he's five years older, not like you and your sister."

"I don't think we'd get along if she was even older than that."

"You should try. My brother is great."

"That's the thing; Claudine isn't."

Danny felt a slight shove as more people tried to get close to the band. He shoved back, but stumbled as he was pushed a little harder.

Luke was now between him and Janelle. Carter was on the other side of her.

Luke and Carter danced more aggressively than Janelle did, swinging their arms and nodding their heads.

Danny backed away. The band wasn't any good. Janelle didn't even notice that he left.

Watching the costume parade was okay for twenty minutes—thousands of little kids dressed as monsters and princesses and rabbits and football players, mixed in with the high school band, the college dance team, and politicians in convertibles.

Danny bought some fried dough with powdered sugar and watched a jazz band that was set up on the median for a few minutes. Then he crossed the street to the Colonial—a century-old theater with wooden seats and high walls and an ornate ceiling. He almost never went there. Half the movies weren't even in English, and the live shows and operas were only interesting to stuffy adults like his father. But during Pumpkin Fest they showed old Looney Tunes cartoons all day for free.

He sat through a dozen Bugs Bunny and Daffy Duck cartoons, laughing the whole time. He was older than most of the kids in the place, but this was a lot more fun than a grunge band. The theater smelled of burnt popcorn.

People were constantly coming and going, grabbing a quick rest or trying to keep bored kids entertained. Parents' patience ran short. Danny decided to move to the front row to avoid the commotion.

There was his sister again, in an aisle seat in the second row. Danny poked her arm as he walked past. She smacked him with the back of her hand.

"Where are all those friends of yours?" Danny asked sarcastically.

"They must be with yours," Claudine replied.

Danny took a seat in the center of the first row. He watched four more cartoons, then headed home for the rest of the afternoon, cutting through the college campus. He imagined what it would be like to have Janelle walking with him, friendly and making jokes.

The sky was overcast and the mist had never quite burned off. As he circled around Brickyard Pond, he felt a touch of loneliness, but he shook it off, like he always did.

His parents weren't home. They'd be strolling among the jack-o'-lantern scaffolds and maybe having a once-a-year ice cream sandwich.

He went up to the bathroom, shut the door, and turned to the mirror. He dropped his left shoulder, then his right, and swirled his fists in a circle as he swayed to the music in his head.

"Now *that's* ridiculous," he said, abruptly stopping his attempt to dance.

He went to the living room and toggled back and forth between three college football games.

A copy of his father's new book was on the coffee table. It was a thin paperback with a photo of the mountain on the cover. Sixty-four pages with one poem per page and a brief intro. The book was dedicated "For my children—May they grow as strong and enduring as the Mountain itself."

Danny read the opening lines of the first poem, "Life in the Shadow."

> *Sixty-one years now:*
> *Twenty-two thousand days*
> *Give or take a few*
> *I've stayed in your shadow*
> *Never out of view.*
> *Your granite peak's a constant reminder*
> *That life's long climb is worth the effort;*
> *That death will not be kinder*

Ooof! Danny thought with a sigh. *You opened the book with that, Dad? Way to be subtle.*

Danny set down the book as a Notre Dame quarterback got sacked by two linemen from USC.

The back door opened. Claudine came in. "What are you watching?" she asked.

Danny thrust his hand toward the screen. "It's called football."

"They showed 'Little Red Riding Rabbit' right after you left," Claudine said.

"Darn," Danny replied. He imitated Red, speaking to Bugs Bunny. "'I got a little bunny rabbit which I'm takin' to my grandma's. Ta *have*, see?'"

Claudine laughed. "'Hey—what sharp teeth ya got, Grandma!'"

Danny nodded. "Good stuff."

"They still out?"

"Seems like it. I never saw them."

"I did," Claudine said. "They tried to get me to walk around with them, but, like, there was no way I was going to be seen hanging out with my parents."

"Seen by who?" Danny asked.

"Duh. Everybody. None of my friends were anywhere near their parents."

Danny stared at the television and decided not to make another remark about Claudine's friend situation. He was surprised that she stood and watched the football game for a minute.

At the next commercial, Danny pointed to the poetry book. "Have you read this?"

"Some."

"The first one is kind of preachy."

Claudine scrunched up her mouth as if deep in thought. "More teachy than preachy, but I know what you mean. That's Dad."

"He's probably read a billion poems in his life," Danny said. "You'd think he'd finally write a good one."

Claudine seemed to be holding back a laugh. "It's a long climb to the peak."

Danny let out a short, huffy breath. "I mean, if you're going to rhyme your poems, at least get the meter right."

"Like you could do better?"

"Like I would want to?"

Claudine went out to the kitchen. Danny heard the refrigerator open. "Do we have any orange juice?" he called.

"Yes," Claudine said.

But when Danny got there, he found only a half-gallon container of carrot juice.

Claudine smirked. "It's very orange, isn't it?"

"Real funny. What normal household has giant cartons of carrot juice and nothing else to drink?" He drank a glass of water instead and went back to the couch.

"Does anything rhyme with Monadnock?" Claudine asked as she looked out the window toward the pond.

"A padlock," Danny said. "A bad doc."

"My dad's sock," Claudine said. "Wow. I guess we could be famous poets, too!"

Danny picked up the book again and leafed through it. A poem titled "Legends of Brickyard Pond" caught his eye. He scanned it. "Here's one that works," he called.

"Let's hear it."

"You can read it yourself. Give me a second." He read it more slowly to himself.

> Unnerved by the sight of phantom steeds
> I stepped aside in the autumn weeds

As the equine rhythm of hooves grew near
And my countenance shook with awe and fear
Now shadow, now flesh, now sinewed hocks
The drown-ed horses of Cheshire Notch
Came racing freely, strong and ripped
No longer bound to their watery crypt
Through the teeth of the storm
A century since death
The four horses raced
With intense, heated breath
Deceased or alive, did it matter which?
For a moment they raced in a spectral niche
Toward an unseen goal with their flying feet
Where they finished the race in a wet, dead heat.

"He saw them!" Danny said.

"Who saw what?"

"The horses. The ghost ones."

Claudine sighed. "If you believe that, you're dumber than I thought."

Danny scowled and looked at the clock: 5:32. He wanted to get a barbecued chicken sandwich at the American Legion booth, and he'd heard that a classic-rock band would be playing in Central Square at 6:00. "If you see them, tell them I left."

"Don't miss Dad's poetry thing. I'm going, so you better."

"I'll be there."

"Don't be late, Danny."

"I can tell time."

"Yeah, and you usually ignore it. You're late for everything."

"What do you care?"

"Just don't be late."

"Just mind your own business and shut up."

He could not possibly look at every pumpkin, but Danny moved slowly through the crowds, amazed at the variety. There were jack-o'-lanterns on every doorstep, on every bench, in every store window, and on hundreds of scaffolds. Every pumpkin had a small candle inside.

In the wide alley between the old inn and the tavern, people were feverishly carving more pumpkins, hoping to push the number above the record.

Central Square was so dense with scaffolds that Danny spent nearly an hour looking at jack-o'-lanterns as the band banged out covers of "Jumpin' Jack Flash" and "Welcome to the Jungle."

Most pumpkins were carved with scary or goofy faces, but others showed intricate scenes of dragons or witches or constellations. *I'll do a better one next year,* Danny thought. *Much better.*

He was surprised by a tap on his shoulder, and more surprised when he turned to see Janelle. She was wearing a maroon baseball cap, and her braid hung down to the middle of her back.

"You disappeared this afternoon," she said.

"Yeah . . . well . . . I had to be somewhere else."

"Too bad. My brother's band was good." She tilted her head toward the bandstand. "This one is just loud."

Danny stared at the band for a second: two guitarists and a drummer in the small gazebo. "You're alone?" he asked.

She nodded. "Luke and them think they're too cool to look at pumpkins. But I love them."

"See this one?" Danny asked, pointing to a fat, round pumpkin on which a carved horse was leaping over a gorge, with a large crescent moon behind it.

"That will look awesome when they light it up," she said. "We've gotta be here for that."

We?

Janelle laughed. "That one makes mine look like something a kindergartner would have done."

"Mine, too. . . . But yours is a whole lot better than mine."

"I didn't see yours. Show me."

"It's way over by the Colonial," Danny said.

"So's mine."

"I know. I saw it." He did not want Janelle to see his very weak pumpkin, so he pointed to a nearby one with fine lines showing a haunted house with a bat flying overhead. "I also did that one," he said, grinning.

Janelle smirked. "You did not."

"Sure I did. It only took a few seconds."

Janelle smiled and swatted him gently on the arm. "Make another one, then. I'd like to see how you do it."

Danny looked around and shook his head. "No tools. And no spare pumpkins."

"They've got hundreds of them in the alley. It only costs a dollar."

"Wish I had the time," Danny said with insincere regret. "Otherwise, I'd make a really elaborate one. A masterpiece."

"Yeah. Me too."

"They're starting to light them," Danny said. The sun was down, and adults with long, tapered candles were lifting pumpkin stems to light the smaller candles inside.

"It's so cool," Janelle said. "Let's get candles and help."

Volunteers were handing them out. Danny and Janelle went from pumpkin to pumpkin, holding the flames to the wicks until they began to glow. All over town, people were doing the same.

"Awesome," Danny said after a third of the jack-o'-lanterns in the square had been lit.

"Let's go see ours," Janelle said. "We'll light them if nobody else has."

She grabbed Danny's arm and gave a little tug. He blew out his candle and they pushed through the crowd, hurrying along Main Street.

A light drizzle was falling, but since there was no wind, the pumpkins were staying lit.

Danny glanced at the clock in the bank as they passed—6:56.

"Oh, man!" he said. "I'm late."

"For what?"

"My father has this . . . show he's doing at seven. I have to be there."

"He's performing?"

"Something like that. But it's all the way over at the college."

"Let's go." Janelle cut down a side street and started running. "We'll make it."

Danny caught up. "You don't have to go," he said. "I don't think you'd want to."

"Is he playing music?"

"No. He's reading his poems."

"Scary Halloween poems?"

Danny rolled his eyes. "I wish."

They cut across the parking lot in front of the diner and

ran past a row of run-down houses rented by college students. They reached the campus in another minute, but the arts center was all the way on the other side.

They ran until they could see it. Danny was slightly out of breath. Janelle did not seem to be. "Think we're too late to get a seat?" she asked.

"Have you ever been in there?"

"Yeah."

"There are about six hundred seats. How many people do you think are going to be at a poetry reading the night of the Pumpkin Fest?"

The head of the English department was at the podium when they walked in, reading an introduction from an index card. Danny quickly counted eleven people in the first three rows of seats. The other rows were empty. He and Janelle stood at the back of the theater and waited.

His mom and sister were in the center of the first row.

"He earned his bachelor's and master's degrees right here at CNSC before taking the PhD at the University of New Hampshire," the introducer read. "And now, please give a warm welcome to Professor Byron Morgan."

Danny's father stepped to the podium at the edge of the stage and everyone clapped politely. Danny led Janelle to the sixth row and they grabbed the first two seats on the aisle.

His father launched right into "Life in the Shadow," which sounded a bit better than when Danny had read it to himself. Then he told a story about the first time he'd hiked to the top of Mount Monadnock with his father when he was eight years old. He mentioned "the exhilaration of seeing a red-tailed hawk from the peak." Then he began reading another poem. "This one is called 'Sighting the Hawk.'"

Claudine glanced back. She stared at Danny and Janelle for a moment, then tugged on her mother's arm. Danny sank lower in his seat as his mother turned in surprise.

At the end of the poem, Janelle leaned toward Danny and whispered, "I loved that line about 'soaring in my father's updraft.'"

Danny winced. "I'd rather be looking at pumpkins," he said. But that wasn't entirely true. He liked that he was being seen with Janelle. At the Pumpkin Fest she'd be part of a crowd and the best Danny could do was trail along behind.

Or maybe not.

His dad read twenty poems, including the one about the brickyard horses, then brought his palms together and stepped to the center of the stage as everyone stood and clapped. Janelle walked toward the front of the theater and lined up behind four people who had copies of the book.

"It's nice that you brought someone with you," Mom said to Danny. "Who is she?"

"She's in my class." He could see Janelle talking to his dad.

"Are you on a date?"

Danny immediately turned red and scowled. "She's just in my class."

Claudine stepped in front of Mom. "Can I go now?"

"I suppose," Mom said. "Be home right after the fireworks."

Claudine left in a hurry. Janelle came back.

Mom reached out her hand. "Hello. I'm Mrs. Morgan."

Janelle reached out, too. "Janelle."

"So," Mom said. "Have you two been enjoying the festival?"

Danny hated that she said "you two," as if they were together. A couple.

"We need to go," he said. "Or we'll miss something."

"Have fun," Mom said.

Janelle said, "Thanks." Danny did not.

"Was I supposed to buy a book?" Janelle asked as they reached the exit.

"No. Of course not."

"I mean, I'd like to have one. But it was twenty dollars."

"I'll get you one. We have boxes of 'em in the cellar."

"That's a lot of money for a little paperback."

"Poems are expensive."

It was still drizzling and there was a bit more breeze. Danny zipped up his jacket.

"I want to see the pond," Janelle said.

Danny pointed. "It's right there."

"I mean, close up."

"Okay."

"I can just picture those horses," she said. "I've heard that legend, but nobody ever described it like your father did. With all those details. I felt like they were galloping right past me."

"I'd like to see them."

"It's exciting and sad. How they died is sad, I mean. The fact that they're still around is exciting."

They walked along the path that circled the pond. No one else was in sight, and only the arts center cast any light on the water. Janelle's moist cheeks glistened.

It was dead quiet. Danny could feel the breeze picking up, but since most of the leaves were down and they all were wet, they didn't rustle.

"Your father has a wonderful imagination," Janelle said. "Such a great way with words. It must be amazing to live with him."

"Amazing," Danny said flatly. "Yeah."

"I can imagine what your dinner conversations must be like. So intelligent and clever."

"Yeah," Danny said. *If you only knew.*

"At my house we just talk about things like who I shouldn't hang out with and why I shouldn't wear ripped jeans or a certain color of lip gloss. My parents are so hung up on appearance. It must be great to have a father who's so deep and . . . worldly."

Worldly, Danny thought. *He's never left New Hampshire for more than ten minutes.*

He let out his breath and watched the mist float away. Here he was, walking with Janelle. Alone in the dark.

Why did his mother have to embarrass him like that? A date? He was lucky that Janelle would even talk to him; he knew he was the nerdiest kid in class. And she was way up there in status, even though she didn't act like it.

"I can't even imagine how exciting it must have been to see those ghost horses," Janelle said. "What did he say, 'strong and ripped'? How cool."

Danny had thought about this more times than he wanted to admit to himself. Walking in the dark with Janelle. Not kissing her or being her boyfriend or anything. Just hanging out. Just knowing that she felt like being with him, too.

He didn't know why he said it; it hadn't even occurred to him that he was about to say it. But suddenly Danny was whispering, " 'How often has my spirit turned to thee.' "

Janelle leaned forward slightly and turned her head to him as they kept walking. "What?"

"Nothing."

"No, really. What did you say?"

"It just popped out of my mouth. Some line my father said." He wished he hadn't said it.

"In one of his poems?"

"No. In somebody else's."

"Tonight?"

"No. Some other time."

"Oh." Janelle was quiet for a moment. "So what was that again?"

Danny sighed and spoke quickly. "'How often has my spirit turned to thee.'"

"To *me?*"

"Thee." Danny kicked gently at a pile of leaves. He could feel his face growing hot. "It just came out." His voice was a little sharper. "It's from William Wordsworth, okay? Some dead poet."

"Okay," Janelle said. She giggled. "It sounded kind of nice."

"It just came out. My father's always saying things like that; quoting poems from a million years ago."

"Like I said," Janelle replied, "he must be amazing to live with."

They didn't say anything else until they'd reached a brighter part of the campus by the library and the science building.

"'How often . . .'" Janelle said. "What was it? 'How often has my spirit turned to thee'?"

"Right." Danny wished they could get off this subject very quickly. "The fireworks will be starting soon."

"You know what Luke said to me this afternoon?"

"No. And I want to get a caramel apple."

"He goes, 'I was thinking about you when I was flossing my teeth this morning.'"

"Why did he say that?"

"I really don't know. I think he was trying to be flattering. Or romantic."

"That must have made you swoon."

Janelle shrugged. "At least he was trying. But it didn't have much impact."

"So, does he like you or something?"

"He seems to be trying to let me think so. The floss thing is the closest he's come to actually saying so, but he shows up wherever I am lately. And he stares at me a lot."

I guess we all do, Danny thought. "So, how would it make you feel if Luke said that his spirit often turns to you—to *thee*?"

"I don't think he's capable of saying anything like that."

"Neither do I."

"But maybe he feels it anyway. Who knows? I think a lot of boys can't say what they feel."

"I'd certainly agree with that."

They'd reached the edge of the campus and could see the biggest scaffold in the distance. It was three stories high, and all of the jack-o'-lanterns were wired with lightbulbs. In the square and the surrounding streets, candles flickered in thousands of pumpkins.

"They're still playing," Janelle said, pointing toward the band. "Let's go!"

She led the way toward the square, where a small crowd was dancing to "Light My Fire."

"Do you dance, Danny?" Janelle asked.

Danny looked around. He didn't see anyone he knew. Not dancing might put a quick end to whatever this was with Janelle. So he said, "I guess I can."

"It's easy." She took a few steps closer to the band, finding an open patch of pavement behind the fountain, but then the song ended with a crash.

"Here's one for the pumpkins!" called the lead singer as the band went into "Monster Mash."

Janelle danced very naturally. Danny danced very awkwardly. But she seemed at least as pleased as she was amused. He started to relax. A little. He was dancing with Janelle; he could even offer to walk her home later.

At the end of the song, the singer said he had bad news and good news. "The fireworks are canceled because of the rain," he said. Everybody booed, but not too much.

"The good news is, we'll play another half hour, unless our equipment gets wet." The gazebo had a roof, but the sides were open.

The music started again. Danny turned to Janelle and found Luke standing between them. He was wearing the same shorts and T-shirt he'd had on at noon, even though the temperature couldn't have been much over forty. There was a tomato-sauce stain near his chest.

Carter was there, too, along with three girls Danny knew but hadn't ever spoken to. The girls were dancing.

Luke leaned toward Danny. "You have no chance," he said.

"With what?"

"You know what." Luke glanced at Janelle. "She's taken."

Danny didn't respond. But who'd been dancing with Janelle? Who'd spent the whole evening with her, looking at jack-o'-lanterns and going to a poetry reading and walking in the dark by the pond? Oh, he had a chance all right. He was way ahead of Luke on this one.

He'd fight this battle. Not with his fists, of course, but with his cleverness and imagination. With his amazing way with words.

Danny stepped past Luke, intentionally bumping against him with a bit of strength. Luke bumped back, sending Danny stumbling into one of the other girls. Danny righted himself and began to dance again.

The girls formed a small circle, and Danny took the spot

next to Janelle, shifting his body to face her. He could practically feel Luke fuming. *Go floss your teeth,* he thought. *Brains beat muscle when it counts.*

Danny tried to think of another great line of poetry to match the "spirit turning to thee" thing. But the band was playing "Monster Mash" again and those lines kept getting in the way.

He was the only guy dancing; Luke and Carter were leaning against the fountain and glaring at him. When the next song ended, Janelle asked, "Did you say something about getting a caramel apple?"

"Yeah." Danny pointed to a white awning set up over a table outside the square. "They sell 'em over there."

"Let's go."

"Where are you going?" called one of the other girls as Janelle and Danny walked away.

"I might be back," Janelle said.

Be cool, Danny thought. *And smart. Show the difference between you and Luke.*

They could hear "Light My Fire" again.

"I guess the band ran out of songs they knew," Janelle said.

"Yeah. They've been at it for more than two hours."

Janelle looked back toward the square. "I don't really want a caramel apple." She kept walking past the booth and headed up Main Street.

"No?"

"Nah. I just wanted to get away from Luke."

To be alone with me? Danny wondered.

"He asked me this afternoon if he could walk me home later," Janelle said. "I said I'd think about it."

"And?"

"I thought about it." She smiled. "He's okay. But he gets kind of . . . grabby, if you know what I mean."

Danny blushed. Janelle obviously was confident that he wouldn't get "grabby." Did she think he was a little kid?

He took a quick look back and saw Luke and Carter trailing behind. The crowds had thinned because of the rain and the cancellation of the fireworks, but there were still a lot of people around.

"So what are we doing?" Danny asked.

"I'm supposed to be home soon," Janelle replied. "You?"

"Pretty soon."

"Let's find another band."

They walked toward Cheshire Tire, where a bluegrass group was playing under the same tent her brother's band had been. A large group of eighth graders was heading toward them, laughing and walking fast. Janelle said hello to a few of them as they passed.

Claudine was behind the group, trying to keep up.

"There's your sister," Janelle said.

"I see her."

They reached the band. Janelle folded her arms and stood still. The rain got harder.

"Did he follow us all the way here?" Janelle asked.

"Luke?" Danny craned his neck and looked around. He spotted Luke and Carter on the other side of Main Street, standing under the awning of the theater.

"They're across the street," Danny said.

"I'm getting cold," she said. "You ready to go?"

"Home?"

"Yeah. Will you walk with me?" she asked, glancing across at Luke.

"Sure." Danny looked uneasily at Luke, too. "Where do you live?"

"Right by the library."

That was easy. From there he could cut behind a church and through the parking lot by the diner, then take a couple of back streets to the campus.

Claudine came walking toward them, very quickly. She veered away when she saw Danny and headed back downtown.

"She was crying," Janelle said.

"She was?"

"Yeah. Should we catch up and see if she's all right?"

Danny stopped walking. "She wouldn't want us to."

"Why not?"

"I don't know. She just wouldn't."

"She's your sister."

"Yeah. That's why."

Janelle squinted and studied Danny. "If my brother saw me crying like that, he'd be there in two seconds."

"We're not like that," Danny said.

"Those kids must have been mean to her."

"It happens."

"It shouldn't."

"Yeah, but it does."

Janelle sighed.

Volunteers were already disassembling the scaffolds, letting the pumpkins roll into the street. Several front loaders were at work, dumping pumpkins into pickup trucks.

"Let's see if ours are still intact," Janelle said.

But the scaffolding by the Colonial was already down. It was just past nine, but the weather was bringing the festival to an early close. They cut behind a block of stores and within seconds were away from the bustle.

Danny tried to think of something to say, but he could tell that Janelle was bothered by his reaction to his sister. He knew Claudine had been crying; she didn't have to tell him that.

So they walked a few blocks in silence.

"What did you say to my father?" Danny finally asked.

"Well, he was busy with the people who wanted their books signed. But I asked him if he'd really seen those horses."

"What did he say?"

"He said he had. More than once."

"He's never mentioned it."

"He wrote that poem about it, so don't act so surprised." Janelle sounded less patient. She'd stopped looking at him.

They waited for a car to back out. The rain looked hard and steady in the headlights, but it was a fine rain, not drenching.

"He first saw them when he was our age," Janelle said. "One night when he was cutting through the woods. There was no arts center then. He thought it was a wind spout or something, or maybe some deer, but then they raced past him and he saw all four of them."

"And they looked like ghosts?"

"They were definitely ghosts. He said he wasn't scared exactly. Not when it was happening. But then he avoided the woods at night for years. So he did get spooked by it."

Danny could already see the library. He wasn't in any hurry to get to her house. "What about the other times?"

"I can't believe you never asked him about this."

"He never brought it up, so how would I know?"

"I guess. Anyway, he last saw them about three years ago. He was in your backyard and they ran on the path around the pond."

"Same kind of night?"

"That's what he said. Rainy and windy."

Janelle stopped and looked up at the streetlight. They'd reached School Street, which did not have a school on it. Hadn't for fifty years.

"You should talk to your dad more," she said. "He's fascinating. Anybody who can write like that . . ."

Danny shrugged. "Some of his poems are pretty good."

"I wish I could write *one* like that."

"You could."

She frowned. "Maybe someday." Janelle looked away and blinked a few times. "Your family doesn't talk to each other much, huh?"

"We talk. We argue."

"You should support your sister more. My brother looks out for me, and it's the best thing in the world to know he's there."

"She's older than I am. She should be looking out for me."

Janelle shook her head gently. "Maybe she would if you did the same."

Janelle was full of advice all of a sudden. "We get along okay," Danny said.

"Doesn't look like it."

Danny wanted to tell her to mind her own business. He swallowed hard. "It's not as bad as it looks."

"I hope not."

Danny shoved his hands into the pockets of his jacket and let out his breath. He looked up School Street. "That way?"

"See that lamppost?" It was halfway up the block, in front of a small brick house.

"Yeah."

"One beyond that . . . I can make it fine from here."

"I'll walk with you."

"It's okay. Thanks for coming this far."

"No problem."

Danny stayed put and watched her walk the fifty yards. She never looked back. He'd have to get home soon, too. But he headed back to Main Street.

Luke was sitting on the steps of the library. Danny crossed the street and circled behind the church to avoid him. But when he reached the parking lot, he could see the library again. Luke was no longer there.

Danny walked faster. The crowds were gone from Main Street, but the cleanup was in full swing. Tents were coming down, trash was being dumped into the backs of trucks, and the ladder of a fire engine was extended to the top of the highest scaffold. A police cruiser sat in the middle of the street; its siren was off, but its blue light was flashing.

Danny felt glum and wished he could settle into a seat at the Colonial Theater and watch more cartoons. But that had ended hours ago. So he'd probably had his last laugh for the day.

Brewbakers Coffee Shop, alongside the Colonial, was still open. It was a place he visited with his mother occasionally. She liked the hippie vibe and the fresh roasted coffee. Danny'd had his fill of junk food today, but a hot chocolate would be nice to kill the chill and maybe lift his spirits.

Claudine had had the same idea. She was in the last booth in the back of the narrow space. She glowered at Danny when he walked in. But he got his drink and slid across from her in the booth. There were only two other customers, at a table by the front window.

"Too bad about the fireworks," Danny said.

Claudine looked down at her mug of chocolate. "Yeah."

Danny blew on his cup, which was steaming hot. Claudine looked more angry than sad. He wanted to ask what had happened, just out of curiosity.

"What's with that girl?" Claudine asked.

"Nothing much. She's in my class. Janelle. Nice person."

Claudine smiled slightly. "Then why does she like you?"

Danny blushed. "She doesn't. Not *like* like. She likes everybody. We just happened to be in the same place for a while."

"But you brought her to Dad's reading."

"I think she just wanted to get out of the rain."

They sipped their drinks for a moment. A Bob Dylan song was playing softly. That was the usual sound track in here: sixties-ish type folk rock all night and day.

Danny swiped a dark drip from the side of his mug and licked his finger. "She liked the reading, though. Said he had an incredible way with words."

"He does . . . sometimes."

"I thought he was pretty good tonight. Too bad the crowd was so small."

Claudine raised her eyebrows. "Tell me about it. Five hundred people watching Daffy Duck this afternoon and he couldn't get twenty for a live performance."

"He didn't seem bothered."

"No. He couldn't have been expecting a big crowd. I thought more faculty would show up, though."

"He made at least one fan."

"Janelle?"

Danny winced and nodded. He hadn't made Janelle a fan of his tonight; he'd said too many unkind things about Claudine.

Neil Young's "Harvest Moon" came on. Claudine took the last swig of her hot chocolate and pushed the mug gently aside.

The door opened and three college guys came in, shaking off the rain. They seemed to know the lone server very well, and joked around with her before ordering coffees. The college students were notorious for having massive parties after Pumpkin Fest, and sometimes for being destructive. Danny had noticed more police out tonight. But these guys looked benign.

"What'd you eat today?" Claudine asked.

Danny went down the list. Everything he'd eaten was either fried or sugary.

"Better not tell Dad," Claudine said. "He'll put you on a lettuce diet for a week."

Danny laughed. Claudine could be funny. Should he ask why she'd been crying? Did it matter?

"You okay?" he asked. It was the first time in his life he'd ever thought to ask his sister anything like that.

"Better," she said. Then she nodded. "Definitely better."

Danny stared into his mug and finished it.

Claudine took out her phone.

"Who you calling?"

"It's almost ten," she said. "Hi, Mom. They canceled the fireworks. . . . Yeah, I'm *with* him. . . . I know, right? We're at the coffee shop. . . . We will. . . . Love you, too."

"What'd she say?"

"She said not to hurry as long we're safe and dry."

"You want something else?"

"No. But maybe we'll just sit here for a while."

This was far more surprising to Danny than the fact that he'd hung out with Janelle for two hours. But they talked about the pumpkins and the poetry and the food, and Danny didn't say a single awful thing the whole time.

Claudine shook her head after a long pause. "We're not normal, Danny."

"No kidding. I was actually quoting Wordsworth tonight when I should have been acting cool."

"What did she think about it?"

"I couldn't tell."

"You should have quoted Bugs Bunny." Claudine sighed and looked away. "Kids can be really mean."

"What happened?"

"Nothing, really. I was just invisible, as usual. We should get home."

Danny grabbed the handles of both mugs in one hand and set them on the counter. "Should we stay on the street or go through the campus?" he asked.

"Campus is nicer," Claudine said. "At least once we get past the dorms."

They walked quietly through the grassy quad and beyond the college library. The rain was steady and the wind was building up, but they'd been warmed by the hot chocolate. Danny was in no hurry to get home.

The arts center was ahead, and the pond.

"'It was the very witching time of night,'" Danny said, quoting "The Legend of Sleepy Hollow." Their dad had read that story to them a hundred times when they were little.

"'Ichabod, heavyhearted and crestfallen, pursued his travel homeward,'" Claudine continued.

"Why do we know those things?" Danny asked. "I mean, every guy I know can tell you the Celtics' free-throw percentage or the Patriots' first-round draft choices for the past twenty years. My head's filled with ancient poetry and short stories."

"Mine, too. That's what we get for having an English professor in the house."

"How'd you like that one about the dead boy in the

churchyard? Did you learn your lesson about what a precious treasure your brother is?"

Claudine laughed. "It would take a lot more convincing than that."

A *thud* on the path ahead of them brought them to a halt. Danny could see what looked like a smashed basketball, or a head.

"It's a pumpkin," he said, kneeling in front of it. He looked around, but they were away from any buildings and the patches of trees were dark.

"It didn't just fall out of nowhere," Claudine said. "Some college kid must have thrown it."

"Watch what you're doing!" Danny said sharply, but there was no one around to direct it to. He lowered his voice. "It's a jack-o'-lantern. Probably from the festival."

They circled past the arts center, then walked along the dirt path toward home. They heard a whistle from the woods.

"Who's there?" Danny said as he stopped.

There was no reply, of course.

"Should we go back?" Claudine asked. "To where it's lighted?"

"Our house is right there," Danny said. They were 250 yards from home.

There was another *splat*, and some wicked laughter. Another broken pumpkin rolled toward them and stopped, its lopsided grin looking more evil in the very dim light.

"Let's go back," Claudine whispered.

"No. Somebody's just trying to scare us."

"Well, they're succeeding," Claudine said. "I know it's not a ghost, but this is not cool."

Danny stood up straight. In a loud, mocking voice, he said, "It must be the headless horseman. Boy, are we ever scared."

There was more laughter. Sounded like two boys. Danny had a good idea who it was.

"Nice try, Luke," Danny said. Maybe Janelle hadn't been impressed with Danny, but Luke had struck out even worse. Of course he wanted revenge.

"Whooo-hoooo-ooo," came the voice from the woods.

"Is that the best you can do, Luke?" Danny replied.

Luke stepped out of the woods with Carter behind him. "I can do a lot better, Danny." He smacked his fist into his palm.

There was another sound now, a soft snort from way behind them. Luke took a step closer. "You got some nerve going off with Janelle," he said. "I told you, you had no chance."

"Looks like you figured wrong," Danny said. "She specifically left because she didn't want to be around you."

Luke balled up both fists and stared at Danny.

"Let us get past," Danny said. "It's late."

"I'll let you go when I'm ready," Luke said.

Claudine chimed in. "Don't be a jerk. Leave my brother alone."

"Stay out of this," Luke said.

"Why? So the two of you can beat him up?"

Luke jutted his head toward Carter. "He'll stay out of it, too." He laughed. "As if I needed help."

Danny was shaking, but he wasn't going to run from Luke. He didn't think there'd be a fight; if Luke beat up somebody as small as Danny, it would turn Janelle against him forever.

But Luke stepped closer and gave Danny a shove. "Stay away from her, you hear?"

Danny stepped forward. "She can choose her own friends."

There was another loud huff, and some scraping at the dirt path about fifty feet away. Danny turned to look. Some drunk college kids?

"Leave my brother alone," Claudine said again.

Luke dropped his fists, but he gave Danny another shove.

"Cut it out!" Danny said, shoving back.

Luke pulled back an arm and flung it, whacking Danny in the shoulder with an open palm. Danny stumbled sideways and fell to his knees. Luke stood his ground.

Something was coming up the path, hard. Danny couldn't quite hear it, but he could sense it. He darted toward the pond. "Move, Claudine!" he shouted.

Claudine scurried to the side. Luke stayed in the center of the path, glaring at Danny. And then his expression turned to horror.

The horses were charging him. Four of them, their hooves pounding the dirt and their tails upraised.

At the last second, Luke dove into the woods, screaming in pain as he landed. He cursed and kicked.

The horses raced away. Danny watched them go, as thin as that morning's mist but as powerful as any storm.

"What the heck was that?" Carter said. He stood with his mouth hanging open, having just barely missed being trampled.

"I cut my hand and sprained my ankle!" Luke said. "Somebody help me."

Danny was still watching the horses. They raced the entire length of the path, then vanished into the woods. His mouth was hanging open, too.

" 'Now shadow, now flesh, now sinewed hocks,' " Danny whispered. "Awesome!"

"What was that?" Carter asked again. "The ghost horses?"

No one answered. Luke stumbled out of the woods, limping badly. He sat down hard on the path and groaned.

"Stay there," Claudine said. "We'll get help."

"We will?" Danny whispered. "Why should we help him?"

"It looks like he's hurt pretty bad."

"He deserves it."

Claudine took a step toward Luke. "We should let you crawl home, but we're not like that. We'll get my dad."

Luke winced with pain and grabbed his leg. "Hurry up."

"That's all you can say?" Claudine said. "How about 'Thank you'?"

Luke said, "Thank you" through his clenched teeth. "What if those horses come back?"

"Duck," Danny said with a sneer.

The rain had finally stopped, and the moon broke through the clouds.

"What's his problem?" Claudine asked.

"He likes Janelle," Danny said. "He *didn't* like the fact that she hung around with me all night."

"I guess Janelle has a brain."

"For avoiding him?"

"Yeah." Claudine stopped at the edge of the yard and looked up at the moon. "And for preferring you, I suppose. . . . Just don't pick your nose in front of her."

"I'll make sure she isn't looking. . . . But she wasn't very impressed with me either."

"No?"

"No. And she was right."

Dad called campus security; then he and Danny went back to the pond. Within minutes, two security guards had helped Luke onto a golf cart. They drove away.

"How did he get hurt?" Dad asked.

"He got scared and jumped off the path."

"I see."

"It was those horses, Dad. They ran right at him!"

Dad nodded. He stroked his chin and scanned the pond. "They're here. Listen."

Danny could hear their soft nickering across the water.

"Very few people have ever seen or heard them," Dad said.

Danny strained to see, but the pond was dark. He headed along the path, hoping to catch a closer glimpse.

"So you saw them at full gallop?" Dad asked. "In all their majesty?"

"They were beautiful," Danny said. "Pure power."

Way in the distance he could hear laughter and yelling, over by the dorms. But close by the only sounds were some dripping from the trees.

"Was that boy picking on you?"

"What makes you ask?"

Dad cleared his throat. "Those horses have been protective of me over the years. They've appeared when I've needed them most."

"Like when you were being chased?"

"Not chased. But . . . down. In need of a lift . . . They're Morgans, you know. A very smart, athletic breed."

There was no sign of the horses when they reached the other side of the pond. No nickering or strong breathing.

"I don't fit in so well," Danny said softly.

"Nor do I," Dad replied. "You don't have to."

Danny nodded.

Dad pointed to the moon and recited:

Upon the moon I fixed my eye,
All over the wide lea;

With quickening pace my horse drew nigh
Those paths so dear to me.

"Wordsworth?"

"Yes."

"You know that girl who was with me? Janelle? She thought your poems were incredible."

"I do what I can. I can't come close to Wordsworth; I know that full well. But that doesn't stop me from trying, from writing in the best way I can."

" 'With quickening pace my horse drew nigh'?"

" 'Those paths so dear to me.' "

Danny watched the water, the small ripples that caught the moonlight for a second. There were a few twitters of birds, a pleasant smell of wet dirt and pond water.

Dad placed his hand gently on Danny's shoulder, then withdrew it. "It's rather cold out here," he whispered. "I'm going to go in."

"I'll be there soon," Danny said. "And Dad?"

"Yes?"

"Thanks."

"For what, Danny?"

"I don't know. The glimmering lake. The spectral niche. Stuff like that."

Dr. Morgan stood still for a moment, and a small smile appeared on his lips. He nodded and walked away.

Danny let out his breath and caught a glimpse of the mist as it swirled away. There was no one near, and very little light. The only awareness was his own, focused on the pond and the cold and the moon overhead.

He shut his eyes and took a deep breath, then walked. The

smashed pumpkin had a huge crack and smelled fresh and strong. From the pond came a short whinny, and Danny could see the horses again, swimming with their heads raised high. They crossed the water and emerged on the other side, just barely visible in the moonlight.

Danny turned for home. He knew that he'd never be lonely again.

RITES OF PASSAGE

The five children of a farming couple all died young—by accident or

by murder. Over the years, the farmer built five barns on his

property, burying a child beneath the floor of each and sealing the

doors off with bricks. According to legend, at least one of those

children has not yet found eternal rest.

"Chase Tavern?" Owen frowned at his friend Mason. "Why would I want to go there?" Chase Tavern had always freaked him out.

"It's a costume thing," Mason said. "The night before Halloween. You dress up like it's Colonial times and dance to old music."

Owen shook his head and slammed his locker shut. "Do you really think that makes it sound better? What am I, five? You expect me to dress up like Ben Franklin or something?"

Mason rolled his eyes and stabbed Owen's scrawny arm with a finger. He was bigger, softer, and way more talkative than Owen.

"There's only one reason we're going," Mason said. "Girls."

"Lots of girls?"

"No," Mason said. "That's the great thing about it. A very select few. And hardly any competition for us from other guys."

Owen walked quickly down the hall. The sun would be setting in an hour and he couldn't wait to get out of school.

"Which girls?" he asked, not turning to see if Mason was following.

"Sophie. Darla . . . *Emma.*"

Owen blushed. "So?" Neither he nor Mason had ever had a girlfriend, or anything even remotely like a girlfriend. But here they were, two months into seventh grade. Maybe it was time.

"That place is haunted," Owen said.

"Everybody says that. So what?" Mason's mouth dropped open. "Which are you more afraid of—girls or ghosts?"

"I'm not afraid of either," Owen replied, although that wasn't true at all. "But what makes you think Sophie and them would have any interest in us?"

"Oh, I don't know," Mason said. "Maybe because Sophie *told* me about it. Practically begged us to come to the thing."

"Us?"

"She knows if I go, you'll go."

"And who else?"

"As if you didn't hear me when I said Emma?"

Owen slung his backpack over one shoulder and shoved open the door. The day was overcast and windy, but he hadn't bothered with a jacket this morning because his mom had dropped him off. It would be a cold fifteen-minute walk home in his T-shirt.

"It's some Daughters of the Revolution thing," Mason said. "You know, a Historical Society event. You dress like it's the 1700s. We might even meet some out-of-state girls from Brattleboro or Massachusetts."

"What good would that do us?" Owen would have been more than happy just to get to know Emma better.

"Are you with me on this?" Mason asked. "I have to let Sophie know by tomorrow."

"What's the rush? It's three days from now."

"It's a very limited party," Mason said. "If I don't say yes tomorrow, she'll get somebody else."

Owen thought it over as they crossed Main Street in front of the Monadnock Savings Bank. Sophie had probably already asked all of the cooler guys and got turned down. "Dressing like it's the 1700s? What does that mean? Buckled shoes with stockings? A powdered wig? We'll be voted geeks of the year if anybody sees us."

"You don't know how girls work," Mason said. "Believe me, it'll be worth it."

Owen stopped on the sidewalk and stared into the China Castle takeout place. The door was propped open with a cinder block and he could smell egg rolls frying. This was where he and Mason usually parted ways, with his friend turning toward the river and Owen continuing on toward his neighborhood across from the college.

Owen smirked. "Emma, huh?"

"And she does *not* have a boyfriend. I checked."

"With who?"

"Sophie."

"You better not have said nothing!"

"Why would I have to?" Mason said. "It's not like you aren't obvious."

"I am not," Owen said.

"Then how do I know that you like her?"

"I never said I did."

"Right. But like *I* said, it's obvious."

Owen let out his breath. "You're very observant. Now I gotta get out of here."

"So you're in?"

Owen shook his head and frowned. "Do we have to dance?"

"We don't have to do anything. But standing around won't get you anywhere."

"What did they do back then? Waltz?"

"Something like that," Mason said. "You just hold her waist and spin her around. How hard could that be?"

Owen was starting to freeze. "I gotta go home. It's wicked cold out here."

"I'll text Sophie to let her know we'll be there."

"I didn't say I would."

Mason was fiddling with his phone. "Hold on," he said to Owen. Then he looked up and grinned. "It's all set. Thursday night. Polish your shoe buckles, man."

Chase Tavern *is* haunted, and some who've been there alone late at night have heard the soft humming of a child or caught a glimpse of wispy gray matter descending the narrow wooden staircase. Sometimes there have been cries of pain, or doors swinging open and slamming shut.

The tavern was built in 1762—more than a decade before the Revolutionary War. It functioned as a taproom, restaurant, and inn for almost a century and then became a private home. Only two families lived there in the many years that followed.

On the death of the last of the Wheelers—who owned the place from 1875 until 1968—it was turned over to the Cheshire Notch Historical Society, which has restored the earlier feel and furnishings and offers occasional tours. Most days the tavern sits empty on its dark, wooded lot toward the lower end of Main Street, its many trees and bushes and a high wooden fence shielding it from the college that dominates the neighborhood.

The tavern's ghostly history is rooted in the two decades

before the Wheelers—when the Gilmans lived in the house and worked the fields beyond it, which later became the site of Cheshire Notch State College.

Henry Gilman married a woman named Ida in 1854. They had five children, none of whom lived past age fourteen.

There was a barn on the property when the Gilmans took ownership. When their oldest child was killed while hunting deer, Henry buried him under the floor of the barn and sealed the door with bricks. He built another barn next to it.

A daughter died a year later. She was buried beneath the second barn, and it, too, was sealed off. A third barn was built.

By 1875, the Gilmans had five barns and four dead children, and there were suspicions that none of the deaths had been accidental. After the fifth death, the Gilmans sold the property and packed up for Massachusetts.

That fifth barn still stands on the Chase Tavern grounds, painted the same brownish mustard color as the tavern's wooden clapboards. The other four barns were demolished long ago to make way for college walkways and green spaces. The legend has become part of the ghostly lore of Cheshire Notch, a town where kids grow up aware of the many spirits in their midst.

Owen scanned the Internet for "Ben Franklin clothing" and found a video of a man dressed as Franklin, explaining that he was wearing a linen shirt, a woolen waistcoat, knee britches, black shoes with a gold buckle, and a tricornered hat.

He found his mother in the kitchen, microwaving dinner.

"Mom," he said, "do I have any linen shirts?" He knew he didn't have a waistcoat or knee britches.

"Why would you want that?" Mom asked. "Something for school?"

"No, this . . . thing I might go to up the street. At the Chase Tavern."

The microwave beeped. Mom lifted out a chicken potpie, jabbed her thumb into the crust, and put the potpie back in. "It won't be crispy, but it'll be done in three minutes," she said. "It would take an hour in the oven."

Owen frowned. "This thing at the tavern? We have to dress like it's the 1700s."

"And it isn't for school?" Mom asked. "And you're actually interested in going?"

"I said I *might*."

"You care about history all of a sudden? You?"

"Do we have a tricornered hat?"

Mom laughed. "We can find one at Walmart, I suppose. With the Halloween costumes. You might find some old clothes and things at the Saint James thrift store. You know where that is?"

"Behind the diner?"

"Try it after school tomorrow."

"Okay."

Owen's mother was a bundle of energy, working long hours in the admissions department at the college and coaching the jumpers and hurdlers on the track team. His father lived all the way over in Manchester, so Owen had a lot of time on his own.

"What's this all about?" Mom asked. "You've never in your life expressed any interest in history. The Chase Tavern is two inches away from here and you've never once asked to go."

"It's just some event. Mason talked me into it."

"What night?"

"Thursday."

Mom pulled out her phone and tapped a few keys. "It says it's a Colonial tea social and dance," she said. She looked at Owen as if he'd gone crazy. "A *tea* social and *dance*."

Owen blushed and let out a sigh. He tapped his fingers on the kitchen table and looked up at the ceiling.

"Okay," Mom said. "I get it." She rubbed the top of Owen's head and kissed it. "Are you going to tell me who she is, or do I have to find out on my own?"

Owen left the house after dinner, feeling lured to the tavern. The building was a hot spot of ghostly energy, and he'd always felt a weird and frightening connection to the place.

It was a three-block walk up to Main Street, then a couple more blocks past college buildings under a canopy of maples and sycamores. Only a few trees still held their leaves, and those that remained had turned to brown or rust.

The picket fence in front of the tavern offered little resistance—it was less than two feet tall. There were no lights on in the building and the grounds were very dark.

Owen stepped over the fence and went around to the side, climbing four brick steps. He tried the door. Locked. He wouldn't have gone in anyway.

He peered through a window with black shutters and twelve rectangular panes. There was the taproom, a narrow area that ran the length of the building—perhaps forty feet. But it was too dark to see much.

Owen had been in there before on school trips; he knew the pine floorboards were wider than any he'd ever seen, and that the room had a fireplace with a brick hearth.

He walked along the dirt driveway toward the barn, which was about fifty feet behind the tavern. The grounds were the size of a football field. He could see a college dormitory in the distance, but things were quiet back here.

The barn wasn't much bigger than a two-car garage. The large doors were thinner than he expected, and the one he pulled open creaked and shook. A damp, grassy smell came to him as he stood in the doorway.

Something scurried toward a corner. Maybe a mouse. Overhead there was fluttering in the loft as a pigeon or a bat moved to safety.

He took two steps onto the dirt floor and looked around, but he couldn't make out anything distinctly in the blackness.

There hadn't been a cow in that barn for seventy years, but the smell of manure was still faintly present. As his eyes adjusted, Owen could make out the shape of a lawn tractor. A wooden ladder leaned against a wall. A wheelbarrow.

And two eyes.

The eyes were gleaming at him from the far corner, but he could see nothing else there. Was it a cat? How were the eyes shining? There was no light to reflect. They were at about his eye level.

The eyes, small and greenish and unblinking, were fixed on him.

Owen took two steps back. He couldn't take his gaze off the eyes. He tried not to sound afraid. "Hey!" he said softly.

The eyes narrowed.

It has to be a cat, Owen thought. He stared for another minute. Then he carefully closed the barn door.

The eyes had looked angry. They didn't seem like a cat's at all.

Owen swallowed, but his mouth had gone dry. He pulled up his sweatshirt hood and tightened the cords; the soft, warm material made him feel more secure.

He walked around the outside of the barn to the back corner. There were no windows in the barn, and he couldn't see any sizeable holes in the walls. But cats were sneaky; they could get in and out of very small places.

He returned to the door and gently pulled it open. The eyes were gone. Owen took a deep breath and headed for the street. He could use a chocolate bar or a giant cookie.

The Citgo station on the corner of Main and Adams has a large, brightly lit convenience store. It was crowded with college students when Owen walked in. Hot dogs were turning slowly on a rolling grill and the local classic-rock station was playing "Dream On" a little too loud.

Owen circled the outer aisles, looking at Twinkies and bags of chips and an entire wall of refrigerated drinks of all sizes and types. He reached for an ice cream sandwich and turned quickly when he heard a chirpy voice saying, "Hi, Owen!"

"Oh. Hi, Sophie."

"My dad's getting gas," she said. Then she laughed. "In the car, I mean. He gets his other gas from beans and beer."

Sophie was pretty. She was only an inch or so taller than Owen, which wasn't much. All four elementary schools dumped kids into the one middle school, so many of his classmates, like Sophie, were new to him. Some were more intriguing than others. Emma, for example.

"That's going to be so cool on Thursday night," Sophie said. She was holding a large bag of barbecue potato chips. "I can't wait."

Owen could wait. But he nodded and said, "Yeah."

"My grandmother's the president, you know," Sophie said. "Of the DAR chapter. That's why I have to go. But it isn't easy convincing people our age how much fun it is."

Owen nodded again. He wasn't convinced yet.

"It's so great that you guys are coming. There's a band: the Monadnock Fiddlers."

"Wicked," Owen said flatly.

"One of my great-great-grandfathers—or even further back than that, I guess—fought in the Revolution," she said. "He marched from Chase Tavern to Boston with the local militia. So I've got a direct connection to that place."

"I was just there," Owen said.

"Recently?"

"Ten minutes ago."

Sophie frowned. "I didn't think it was open."

"It's not. I was just looking around."

Sophie raised her eyebrows and smiled. "You were trespassing."

Owen shrugged. "Was I? It's not like there's a sign or a guard or anything."

Sophie's face brightened. "Oh, it's guarded." She touched Owen's arm, then pulled her hand away. She lowered her voice, practically hissing the next word: "Spirits."

"Sophie?" A man was standing by the entrance, beckoning to her.

"Gotta go," she said. "Coming, Dad!"

Owen looked at the ice cream sandwich. He'd squeezed it hard when Sophie touched his arm. It was dripping out of the wrapper already and his hand was sticky. Should he put it back and get another one?

He gingerly gripped the sandwich in his other hand and wiped the sticky one on his sweatshirt. Then he paid for it and ate it on the walk home, alternating biting it and wiping his mouth with his sleeve.

*   *   *

At sunrise on April 21, 1775, twenty-nine minutemen set out on foot from the Chase Tavern, headed for Lexington and the fight for independence from British rule. They were led by Captain Eleazor Chase. A plaque on the tavern's outer wall commemorates the occasion. It was posted by YE CHESHIRE, NH, CHAPTER DAUGHTERS OF YE AMERICAN REVOLUTION.

Just less than one hundred years after those soldiers departed, a thirteen-year-old girl sat weaving in the former tavern's sewing room, intricately working the foot pedals of a wheel as she fashioned a brown and scarlet rug. The room's walls were painted dark red, and the boards beneath her feet were wide and scuffed and gray.

The February day was cold, and a fire burned in the sewing room's brick fireplace.

She could hear her mother crying in the adjoining kitchen, so she rose to comfort her. The girl's young brother had drowned a few months before, crashing through thin ice on a nearby pond as he and their father were hunting waterfowl. He was the fourth of the Gilman children to die, and the latest tragedy seemed too much for Mrs. Gilman to bear.

Bread was baking in the small oven built into the brick wall adjacent to the hearth, and it smelled as if it might be overdone. The girl removed the bread; its crust was dark and slightly scorched, but it would be all right.

Mrs. Gilman sat in a black wooden chair, her face in her hands. The girl placed a comforting hand on her mother's shoulder.

"Let her be, Charity," her father said sternly, appearing in the outer doorway. He had returned for his noon meal.

The girl returned to her weaving. She tried to block out

151

the harsh words her father was whispering in the kitchen. She tried not to hear her mother's sobs.

The kitchen door slammed. The girl looked up in surprise.

A moment later, her mother heard her scream. It was the last sound the girl ever made.

"Did you see the way she was looking at you in English?" Mason asked as he and Owen headed for the cafeteria.

"Who was what?"

"Emma. She's looking forward to the party. She knows that you like her."

Owen hadn't seen Emma look his way at all. He elbowed Mason hard in the ribs. "How would she know that?"

"Everybody knows it."

"Get out." Owen grabbed a tray and sized up the lunch line. Chicken fajitas and corn.

"It isn't *real* chicken," Mason said.

"So what? I'm hungry." Owen pushed his tray along and grabbed a carton of chocolate milk and a banana. "What'd you say to Emma?"

"I didn't say nothing. Just that we'd try to get there early so we'd be sure to get free cookies and stuff. She said she's looking forward to dancing, so watch out."

"She said 'watch out'?"

"No. *I'm* saying watch out. Be prepared to dance."

"You better, too."

"Count on it."

"With who?"

"Darla, I hope."

"I thought you liked Sophie?" Owen asked.

"I do. But I like Darla better."

Owen and Mason took seats in a corner of the cafeteria. Across the way, Sophie and Emma and Darla were at a table with the cooler crowd, including several boys. Owen turned his head so it looked like he was gazing out the window, but he shifted his eyes over toward Emma: soccer player, light brown ponytail, tough-but-sweet smile, great sense of humor.

"Thursday night, everything changes," Mason said. He picked a tiny cube of tomato out of his fajita and wiped it on his tray. "We take several steps up in status, Owen. Just for being brave enough to look like idiots."

"As if that's something new?"

"*Colonial* idiots," Mason said. "Girls love that sort of thing."

The St. James thrift shop was below street level in an old stone building. A bell tinkled as Owen opened the door, and he smelled old clothes. Racks of dresses and women's coats filled the small space. A short gray-haired woman at the counter smiled and said, "Hello there. We have some children's clothes in the back."

Owen just said, "Okay," but he looked around until he spotted a section of men's items. He flipped through a rack of sports coats until he found a black vest. It didn't look particularly old, but it might do over a white shirt.

The vest was big for him, but it was the only one like it.

Owen was the only customer. The woman asked if she could help.

"I was looking for some old-fashioned stuff."

"For Halloween?"

"Sort of. There's this party . . ."

"At the Chase?" The woman seemed delighted. "I'll be there. Serving punch. I'm a member."

"Oh."

"The children's party is one of the highlights of the year," she said. "Oh, I shouldn't say 'children.' Young men and ladies."

"Right."

The woman reached for the vest and held it up. "This will do just fine," she said. "You can tighten it from behind with the laces. See?"

"Yeah."

"It's so nice that you'll be attending. We haven't had enough boys show up in recent years."

Owen nodded. That was no surprise.

"I have a black string tie at home that would be perfect with this vest," the woman said. "My husband used to wear it at events like this one, but he passed away last year. I'll be glad to let you use it."

"Okay."

"You can pick it up here tomorrow after school. All right?"

"Thanks." Owen didn't ask about gold-buckled shoes or knee britches. He figured a pair of black pants and his regular shoes would be fine.

He paid three dollars for the vest. "It all goes to charity," the woman said.

Owen sifted through a pile of fishing magazines on a table near the checkout. The bell rang again, and Sophie walked in.

"Hi, Grandma," she said. "And hello, Owen."

"Hi, Sophie," they said, almost in unison.

"So you know each other," the woman said.

"Owen's coming to the party," Sophie said.

"I got this vest," Owen said, holding it up for Sophie.

"Nice." Sophie fiddled with some cheap bracelets in a basket. She picked up a light blue one and put it on her wrist, then placed it back in the basket. "Any good merch come in?" she asked her grandmother.

"Probably nothing that would interest you." Then she tilted her head toward Owen and winked at Sophie. "Well, something nice *did* just come in a few minutes ago."

Owen blushed. Sophie giggled.

"Alas, Grandma. He has his eye on someone else."

Owen looked down at the floor and bit his lip. "Who says?"

"Oh, *I* don't know," Sophie replied. Very softly she sang, "Emma, Emma, Emma."

Owen rolled his eyes.

"You'll look dashing in that vest," the woman said.

"Emma's the lure," Sophie said. "She's the only reason Owen agreed to go."

Owen blushed deeper. "I'd better get home." He could hear Sophie and her grandmother giggling as he left.

On at least three occasions in the past twenty years, the Cheshire Notch Fire Department has been summoned to the Chase Tavern to investigate reports of smoke coming from the chimney. But they've never detected a sign of a recent fire.

There are eight fireplaces in the tavern, and all are connected to a single, central chimney. Downstairs are the large hearth in the taproom, smaller ones in two parlors, and the main one in the kitchen. Each of the four upstairs sleeping areas has its own fireplace. For safety reasons, none of the eight has ever been lit in the years since the Historical Society took charge of the building.

But smoke is occasionally seen, and the smell of burning wood is sometimes very apparent.

Interviewed by the *Daily Sentinel* a few years back, the fire chief speculated that the "smoke" must have been steam that was rapidly evaporating from the slate roof after a storm. He also said cooking smells and other odors can linger in wooden beams for years and be activated when warmed by intense sunlight.

Privately, the chief told friends that upon entering the tavern's kitchen after midnight one very cold January night, he surprised a man and two young boys sitting by a roaring fire, eating what appeared to be rabbit or deer meat from wooden bowls. When he flicked on a flashlight, the people and the fire disappeared.

The night of the dance, Owen hesitated on the tavern's brick walkway and fussed with the string tie, which pinched his throat a little. He could hear fiddle music and see a few people through the taproom window.

"Come *on*," Mason said. "We're already late."

A woman in a blue gown with white ruffles and frills greeted them at the door. "Welcome to 1772," she said. "It's all right to keep your hats on tonight."

Owen's eyes went right to Emma, who was near the punch bowl, laughing with some boy Owen didn't recognize.

He quickly counted thirteen girls and six boys, plus him and Mason. Sophie's grandmother was behind the punch table, and two fiddlers and a woman with a mandolin were in the corner, playing their instruments.

The room was lit by electric candles in wall sconces, so the wide pine boards of the wall and floor were dimly lit. The only kids Owen recognized were Sophie, Emma, and Darla.

"Who are these people?" he whispered to Mason.

Mason shrugged. "Out-of-towners, I guess."

Some of the kids had elaborate costumes—buttoned jackets and stockings—but most of the girls were wearing plain dresses with long sleeves and simple white bonnets.

There were plates of cookies by the punch bowl, so Owen went over. Sophie's grandmother told him he looked very handsome.

The music sounded way more classy than Owen had expected from fiddles—rising and falling lightly and with precision. He swayed a little and felt giddy, as if he was suddenly in a more respectable era. He immediately felt older. He eyed Emma, but she didn't look his way.

Sophie and Darla came over. "Isn't this fun?" Sophie said, touching Owen's wrist.

"Just got here," Owen said. "I wouldn't say it's fun yet." But he smiled and bit his cookie, which was spicy and had walnuts and raisins. Some powdered sugar drifted onto his vest.

"No one's dancing," Darla said. She poked Mason's arm. "The boys are always shy at the beginning."

"I'm not shy," Mason said. He gave her a big grin. "I just don't see anyone I want to dance with."

Darla stuck her tongue out at him. Mason smirked. He put out his palm, gesturing toward the open space near the band. Darla laughed and they stepped out to dance.

Darla took the lead and Mason awkwardly tried to follow. Owen took a step back toward the wall. He could never dance like that in front of a crowd. This evening was going to be a disaster.

Sophie was humming. She looked up at him. "Would you like to dance, Owen?"

"Maybe in a little while." Owen was starting to sweat. "I'll . . . watch."

"It isn't hard," Sophie said.

"I know." He couldn't believe Mason had jumped right into it. Everybody in the room was watching him and Darla twirl around.

Sophie turned to Owen. "Mason has a lot of energy."

Owen nodded. Mason had been so sure he'd make a breakthrough with Darla tonight, getting her to like him. He'd certainly moved quickly.

Emma was still laughing with that other guy, who looked a little older and quite strong. If Owen danced with Sophie, would it give Emma the wrong impression? He didn't want her thinking he was off-limits.

So he took another step back and leaned against the wall.

"He was here last year," Sophie said.

"Who was?"

"That guy you're worried about." Sophie jutted her chin toward Emma and the boy. "He's from Peterborough. Eighth grader."

Owen felt about two feet tall. When the next song started, Emma and the boy stepped onto the dance floor.

In a few minutes, another guy Owen didn't know came over and asked Sophie to dance. She glanced at Owen, then nodded eagerly and followed him onto the floor.

Owen grabbed three more cookies.

The girls who didn't have partners were dancing in a circle. Some of them kept looking over at him. He kept eating cookies and drinking apple-cider punch from a blue-and-white teacup.

He tried not to stare at Emma and her partner. The boy seemed confident and talkative and muscular and mature—everything Owen wasn't.

158

He watched the dancers for half an hour. When the band leader called everyone onto the floor for lessons, Owen left the taproom and cautiously climbed the wooden staircase.

There was only one small light lit on the entire second floor. Owen entered a room that was directly above the taproom, with dark, wood-paneled walls. A white pitcher rested on a small wooden stand, and a cradle sat in the corner.

The upstairs was split into four rooms, each with a bed and its own fireplace. Large beams ran the length of the ceiling and small woven rugs covered parts of the pine floors. There were quilts hanging from racks and several wooden dressers.

Mason probably wouldn't even miss him if he left. Emma certainly would not. He pulled a wooden chair away from the wall in the front bedroom and sat by the window for a long time, looking out at the street.

The stairs creaked a bit on his way down, but the music was loud enough that no one heard. He ducked into a parlor on the other side of the house and thought about whether he should leave.

"Hello," came a soft voice.

The only light in the room came from an electric candle in the window. Owen squinted. A girl around his age was sitting on a sofa.

"Don't you like to dance either?" Owen asked.

"I've never danced with a boy my age," she said.

Owen sat at the edge of the sofa, as far from the girl as he could. "It feels kind of silly," he said. "I think I'd make a fool out of myself."

The girl was wearing a light blue corset over a white dress, and she had the same type of bonnet the other girls were wearing. "I'm sure you wouldn't look foolish," she replied. "When everyone is dancing, they're not very concerned about how anyone else looks. The steps aren't difficult."

It was odd how different this room felt from the taproom. A lively party was going on right across the hall, but this little parlor seemed so quiet and serene. "I'm Owen," he said. He held out his hand.

She didn't shake it, but touched his palm lightly with her own. "I'm Charity."

Owen fumbled for something to say. "The cookies are good."

Charity smiled.

"The punch is, too. Do you want some?"

Charity shook her head. "I can teach you the dance steps," she said. "In here. Once you've learned, you won't feel so self-conscious about joining the party."

Owen blushed, but he doubted she could see that in the dim light. He looked at the floor. "All right," he finally said.

They stood, and Charity held out her hands, which were warm. She pulled Owen toward her, then whispered, "Watch my feet." She moved her right foot to the side, then swept her left foot over to meet it, then stepped the right one back and moved the left one to join it. "It's a simple box step," she said. "The most basic of all. Just follow me."

Owen stumbled a couple of times, but it didn't take long for him to get it.

"At the end of each box cycle, let's twirl," Charity said. She put her left arm on Owen's shoulder and held her right hand higher. She smelled slightly flowery, like talcum powder. "See how easy?"

It wasn't easy, but Owen felt much less foolish now that he had some idea what to do. The musicians began a livelier tune, and Owen grew more confident. No one could see them. It was fun.

There was plenty of room for just two dancers in the parlor, so they circled the entire room, doing box steps and twirls. Owen was grinning and Charity seemed very happy. He was glad he hadn't left. Their faces were close; he could smell the warmth and life of her hair. He could feel the slight sweat of her hands.

When the song ended, he heard Mason laughing and several kids clapping in the doorway. Owen turned and blushed, but he was smiling.

Mason folded his arms. "What are you doing, bro?"

"We were dancing."

Owen could see Sophie and Darla laughing hysterically behind Mason. "What's so funny?"

"Are you nuts?" Mason asked. "The party's over here."

"I know," Owen said. "We're on our way."

"We?"

"Me and Charity. We were practicing in here first."

Mason's mouth was hanging open. "Owen," he said, "you all right?"

Owen suddenly realized that Charity had left the room. "Where'd she go?"

"Where did who go?" Mason asked.

Owen didn't answer. He walked to the parlor's back doorway and said, "Charity?"

"You're not fooling anybody," Mason whispered sharply. He grabbed Owen's arm. "Are you crazy? Dancing by yourself in the dark?"

Owen sputtered. "I wasn't by myself. She was right here."

"Dude," Mason said, "if you're going to dance with an imaginary girlfriend, at least do it in private."

"I was dancing with a girl."

"No, you weren't."

Yes, I was, Owen thought. He pushed Mason aside, went out the front door, and stormed toward the back of the building. He'd touched her; she was warm and real.

Tree branches blocked much of the sky, but he could see stars overhead and feel the breeze on his face. He climbed the back steps and rattled the kitchen door, but it was locked.

Owen shuffled through the dry leaves and opened the barn door. He didn't know why. He took a quick look inside, then pushed the door closed and stepped onto the grass, finding a clear spot to look at the stars.

He let out his breath. Then he grabbed his tricornered hat and tossed it aside and kicked it. He was gentler with the tie, since it didn't belong to him, but he took it off and pushed it into his pocket.

And then he heard footsteps.

"Owen?"

"Charity."

She was on the dirt path, about ten feet away. "Thank you for the dance, Owen," she said.

"Where'd you go?" he demanded. "You left me looking like a jerk when my friends came in. They thought I was dancing by myself."

At least he could save face if she'd return to the taproom with him. Mason and the others would see who he'd been dancing with.

"I couldn't face them," she said.

"Why not? Come inside with me."

"I'm sorry, but I cannot," she said.

"Charity—" he began, but the girl was fading away. He could see the barn behind her—he could see it right through her!

"I must be leaving," she said. And within seconds she was gone.

Owen wanted to run, but he was too afraid to move. He stared at the spot where Charity had been. How could a ghost have been so solid, so real? How had he held her and spun her around and smelled her hair and her skin?

He stared at the spot for what seemed like an hour. Then he backed away, keeping his gaze there. When he reached the tavern, he turned to the street and kept walking.

He was sweating. His skin felt feverish, but inside he was chilled to the bone.

Owen nodded off a few times that night, but he never slept for more than a solid minute. Each time he fell asleep he felt Charity's touch, then jolted awake as he watched her fade away. He turned on a light in the hallway and kept his door open.

He begged off school the next morning, partly because he felt awful and partly because he was too embarrassed to face Mason and Sophie and the others.

"I'll stop back on my lunch hour," Mom said. "Stay in the house. Eat something besides potato chips."

"No problem."

"And don't touch those candy bars. They're for the trick-or-treaters."

"Right." Owen had forgotten that it was Halloween.

He was able to sleep a little better now that it was daylight. He got up at ten thirty and had a bowl of cereal, then watched TV and ignored a few texts from Mason.

8:57 a.m. you sick?
9:02 a.m. you there?

9:48 a.m. you sick?
10:41 a.m. can you go out tonite?
10:43 a.m. we r trickrtreating
10:43 a.m. sophie darla emma too
10:44 a.m. you there?

So Mason's plan had seemed to pay off, at least for him. They hadn't been trick-or-treating since fourth grade, but now it was apparently cool again, as long as you had girls along. Owen wasn't about to give them something more to laugh at. He was certain everyone at school had heard by now that he'd been dancing by himself in the dark.

An Internet search for "Chase Tavern ghosts" came up empty, but Owen tried to dig deeper. "Cheshire Notch ghosts" yielded stories about an unhappy spirit in a dilapidated old chapel at Woodlawn Cemetery, the haunted dorm at the college, and the famous Horses of Brickyard Pond.

Scrolling down, he found some vague recollections of sightings at the Chase Tavern. And then a link to "Gilman Murders."

The entry was brief but chilling.

In the late 1800s, a man named Henry Gilman alleg-edly murdered his own five children over a period of several years, burying each one in a separate barn on his property in Cheshire Notch, N.H. Each of the deaths was made to appear to be accidental, includ-ing the misfiring of a gun, a drowning, and a fall into a burning fireplace. Gilman's wife fled to a relative's home in Massachusetts after the fifth death, and Mr. Gilman left the area without a trace. Several of the Gilmans are said to haunt the home, which now operates as a museum under its original name, the Chase Tavern.

"Charity Gilman," Owen said aloud. He stared at the screen, then read the entry again. He typed Charity's name into his search engine. Nothing that was the least bit relevant came up.

He sent a text to Mason.

> 1:31 p.m. cant go out. sick.

The reply came almost two hours later:

> 3:27 p.m. your not sick. suck it up and come with us.

There was a steady stream of trick-or-treaters after six o'clock, and Owen handed out candy bars to little kids in costumes for an hour. When he saw Mason and the girls coming up the block, he ducked inside and told his mother he was going to take a shower.

"I'll take over," she said. But no sooner had Owen got to his bedroom than she called up to tell him that his friends were out front.

"Tell them I don't feel good!"

"Come and tell them yourself."

Owen looked into his mirror and let out a sigh. He wiped his hair away from his forehead and checked his shirt for food stains. Then he went back downstairs.

Mason was in the doorway with a red bandanna around his head, tied at the side like a pirate, and a black eye patch. "Avast, matey!" he said.

"Yeah, right. Avast," Owen mumbled.

"Hi, Owen," said Sophie, who was standing on the front steps. Darla and Emma waved and said the same thing. They all had tiaras and bright red lipstick.

"Come with us," Sophie said. She shook her duffel bag. "Lots of candy!"

Mom put her hand on Owen's shoulder. "Go ahead," she said. She even gave him a little push. "I can handle the kids alone."

Owen frowned. "Give me a minute," he said. "I don't have a costume."

"Just put on a funny hat," Mason said. He raised his eyebrows and jutted his head slightly toward the girls.

Owen had left his tricornered hat on the ground outside the tavern last night.

Mom was opening a closet in the front hall. She took out an orange-and-black knit cap with long ear flaps. "Try this," she said. "It looks goofy enough."

They hit the other houses on Owen's street, then circled along the back streets near the river. They joked about some of their teachers and other kids in class. No one mentioned the dancing.

Coming down a flight of steps, Sophie dropped a bag of M&M's. The others kept walking.

"Hold up, Owen," she said.

Owen waited.

"I think we've got plenty of candy," Sophie said. She walked very slowly, letting the others get ahead. "So . . . what happened last night?" she asked.

"You really want to know?"

"Yes." Sophie stopped at the corner. "Believe me, I know all about that place. I've seen a ghost there."

"A girl about our age?"

"No. Just a wispy thing that didn't have a lot of shape. But it was definitely a presence. It knew I was there."

"Was it trying to scare you?" Owen asked.

"I think so. I do. It didn't say 'boo' or anything clichéd like that, but I was sure it wanted me to leave."

Mason, Darla, and Emma were more than a block ahead now. Owen had no desire to catch up. "Were you alone?"

Sophie shook her head. She started walking again, up toward Main Street. "I was there with my grandmother. We were straightening things up after giving a tour, so it was pretty late and everyone else had left. She was in the kitchen and I went upstairs. I'm not sure why I did, but I felt very curious. So I went to the front bedroom—to the right when you get up there—and I sat on a chair. And I felt this ice-cold draft, as if a window was open, but I checked and none were. But when I'd checked the last window, I felt like I was trapped, like there was something between me and the stairs. And then this mist started taking shape and it just hung there, all grayish and slightly shiny."

"The girl last night wasn't like that at all," Owen said. "She was like a real human until the end. Then she faded away, but even then you could tell she was a person."

"Wow," Sophie said. "I've never heard of such a clear image there."

"It was way more than an image," Owen said. "We were dancing. She was solid. We *talked*."

Sophie whistled. "Let's go," she said.

"Now? It's open?"

"No . . . But I know how to get in."

* * *

167

Ida Gilman could find no relief from her sadness. Five children, all of them dead, and a husband who offered no sympathy or remorse.

A cousin in Massachusetts offered to take her in, to get her away from the scene of her everlasting grief.

Henry wanted no part of it. But rumors of murder persisted, and he was shunned by the neighbors. When talk of an investigation mounted, he abruptly sold the farm. He and Ida packed up the possessions they wished to keep and told almost no one where they'd be heading. His plan was to slip out of town and disappear.

Privately, Ida confided that she wished she could go to her cousin's without Henry, to leave him behind. Who needed a constant reminder of the horrible things she'd always known he'd done? He'd ruined everything that had ever given her joy.

But he ruled, and he said he was going with her. She knew there was no sense in arguing. She knew that he would kill her if she objected.

The overcast sky made things even darker than the night before as Owen and Sophie approached Chase Tavern. Every light was out.

"The kitchen door?" Owen whispered.

Sophie shook her head. "The cellar."

Toward the far back corner of the tavern was a hatch-type cellar door, the kind that lies at an angle and opens up to reveal a set of steps. This one was rusted and was held in place with a couple of cinder blocks.

"It's just a crawl space," Sophie said. "You have to squat, but we can make it to the inside door and get upstairs. The lock is rusted out, so all we have to do is remove the cinder blocks."

Owen did that, then lifted the rickety hatch. He could feel cobwebs and smell the dampness of the basement. It was pitch-black down there. He tried to remember where the door from the kitchen to the cellar was. He figured if they stayed close to the back wall, they'd get to it.

"What's the floor like?" he asked. His heart was beginning to race.

"Hard-packed dirt," Sophie said. "There are some support poles, but not much else to trip over. Just go slowly."

Owen let her lead the way. "Should I leave this open?" he asked, pointing to the hatch.

"Close it," she said, "so no animals come in. Just don't let it slam."

Owen carefully lowered the hatch, then tested it to make sure it didn't stick. He touched the wall and scuffled along in a squat.

There were four wooden steps in the corner, and they led to a door that opened into the kitchen. The small amount of light from outside offered much more visibility after those minutes in the cellar.

"Careful," Sophie whispered. "There are breakable things all over. Pitchers and vases and things."

Owen put his hands close to his sides. They stood in the kitchen for a minute, listening. But there were no sounds inside the house.

"She was in there," Owen said, gesturing toward the door to the parlor.

"Was she?" Sophie said with a light laugh.

"She was," Owen said.

Sophie touched Owen's arm. "I believe you, remember?"

They sat on the sofa and Owen tried to steady himself. After five minutes, he said "Charity?"

There was no indication that she or any other ghosts were present.

"Do we dare go upstairs?" Sophie asked.

Owen thought for a moment, then said okay.

The stairs had one tight turn. Owen thought he smelled talcum powder.

"I love this room," Sophie said as they entered the biggest of the four upstairs rooms—the one where she'd seen the mist. "It was the main sleeping area for travelers way back then."

They checked all of the rooms, but it was too dark to see much. Every shadow seemed ghostly.

"Let's just sit here," Sophie said. "Real quiet."

Owen slid to the floor with his back against the wall. Sophie sat next to him. "Are you scared?" she whispered.

Owen thought about how to answer. "Yes, but I don't want to leave," he said. "It feels like something's going to happen, you know?"

He had tried all day to rationalize what he'd seen, wondering if he'd somehow been dancing with a real girl and that she'd run off out of shyness when Mason and the others came by, and had spoken to him in the tavern yard but hadn't really faded away, but just appeared to because the moonlight and the wind were playing tricks with his eyes.

But he knew better than that. He knew what he'd seen.

And here he was, with an actual, live girl, who seemed to get it and was cool and very brave to be sitting in a haunted tavern at night when she wasn't supposed to be in here.

So if Charity did come floating into the room, he wouldn't be alone. He would know he wasn't crazy.

They sat there for half an hour. Every tiny creak or flash of light from the street made Owen's heart jump, but nothing suspicious happened.

Sophie said they'd better get going.

"Can we go out a real door?" Owen asked.

"No," she said. "We can't risk being seen going out the front. And the kitchen door only locks from inside. We have to use the cellar again."

They made their way through the taproom and the kitchen and onto the cellar steps. As Owen reached behind to close the door, it slammed shut on its own.

"Quiet," Sophie hissed.

"That wasn't me," Owen said. "I didn't touch it."

They stared toward the door, though it was too dark to see anything down here. Owen listened hard for footsteps. There was nothing.

He started shaking. "Must have been the wind," he said.

"Not in the building!"

"Well, something slammed the door."

"Don't panic, but let's get out of here."

They made their way back along the wall. Owen pushed up on the hatch. It wouldn't budge. "You've gotta be kidding me," he said.

"Push harder," Sophie said.

Owen did. The door was tight and heavy. "Man," he said. "I don't want to go back upstairs."

"Me neither." Sophie laughed nervously. "Whatever slammed that door wouldn't be too happy to see us."

Owen didn't think that was funny. He pushed at the hatch again, then smacked it with his fist.

"Ow."

"Let me try." Sophie put both hands on the door and tried to shake it. "Help me here, Owen."

The door finally gave way, and they scrambled into the yard. Owen replaced the cinder blocks and they backed toward the barn.

"That hatch was barely closed when we went upstairs," Owen said.

Sophie squeezed Owen's forearm. "Something messed with it. I told you the place was haunted."

Owen nudged her. "You didn't have to tell me, remember? I lived it last night."

"Yeah, but I don't think that girl would try to trap us like that, do you?"

"No. She was nice. I hope she doesn't have to cope with evil ghosts all the time in there."

As they passed the side of the tavern, Owen saw a glimmer in an upstairs window. "Look," he said. Something appeared to move behind the glass.

"It's because all the panes are different," Sophie said. "Some are very old and others are newer, so they catch the light differently. It gives the appearance that something's there."

Owen kept staring. Something faint but substantive seemed to be in that upstairs room, looking out. It shifted to the right, then the left.

And then Charity's face appeared. She was there for the briefest instant, and then she was gone.

"Did you see her?" Owen asked.

"See who?"

"It was Charity. I'm sure of it."

"Well," Sophie said, "I'm not going back in to find out."

Owen watched for movement but couldn't see anything

else behind the glass. A car drove by on Main Street, and he saw that the light was reflected differently from every pane.

So maybe he hadn't seen Charity tonight. But he did want to see her again soon.

What about those other four barns?

Owen couldn't help but wonder. There was no sign of them on the tavern property, but he knew that it had once been a much larger farm. He'd asked Sophie, but she'd never heard of the other barns or the Gilman murders.

Had Charity been murdered by her father? If she had, then which barn had she been buried in? He had no way of knowing; the single paragraph he'd read on the Internet hadn't provided those details. And how could you trust a flimsy report like that?

Early Saturday morning he cut through the college grounds to a spot behind the tavern. He was in direct sight of a dormitory but in a half-acre patch that was overgrown with brush and trees. It appeared that it had never been developed in any way.

There were a few empty bottles and some other trash, but no signs of recent activity. Owen walked slowly through the brush, looking for stones or bricks that might have been part of a foundation.

And then he found them. Several large stones that formed a low triangle, apparently the corner of an old building. They were shielded by thick weeds. He could see the existing barn through the slats of the tavern's wooden fence, and this corner lined up precisely with the barn.

So, if the five barns had been in a straight row, this was the only one that could still have a trace. The other spots would have been cleared for the dormitory's lawn long ago.

Owen stepped off what might have been the rest of the barn's footprint, but he saw no other signs of it. Just these stones. Was there a body buried a few feet away? Were there three more right out there under the lawn?

He sat on the stones and felt the breeze on his face. A late maple leaf drifted down.

Such a peaceful place, he thought. *At least in daylight.* But what had happened here a century and a half before? Could he ever know?

Would Charity's ghost know that she'd been murdered? If she was his age now, then had she stayed that same age for all these decades? If you're thirteen when you die, do you stay that way forever?

*   *   *

mason347: hang out later?

owen^B: ok

mason347: you spooked?

owen^B: not

mason347: herd your seeing ghosts

owen^B: who said?

mason347: who you think?

owen^B: whatd she say?

mason347: you saw a dead girl in the window

owen^B: might have

mason347: go there tonite?

owen^B: maybe to the barn.

mason347: ok but shift your focus to a LIVE girl, man. she likes you.

owen^B: emma?

mason347: no stupid. open your eyes

His mom was spending the afternoon putting the jumpers through some preseason drills. She'd left Owen a note and a ten-dollar bill, telling him to get something to eat downtown.

The previous Saturday, Main Street had been mobbed with people for the Cheshire Notch Pumpkin Fest. Today was much quieter. The sounds of televised football games poured out of the bars, but the ice cream place was closed for the season and the coffee shops were nearly empty.

Owen sat on a bench outside the Colonial Theater and tried to decide what to eat. A hamburger from Local Burger? Chicken fried rice? A couple of slices of pizza? Main Street was loaded with places to eat, and plenty of the spots were inexpensive, to draw in the college students.

Sophie liked him? How would Mason know that? He'd been so wrong about so many things for so long that the only way he could know that was if Sophie had told him directly. Two days ago Mason said *Emma* liked him, and that had obviously been untrue. Mason just wanted Owen to play along to help him advance his cause with Darla.

A hamburger sounded good. With hand-cut fries. He crossed Main Street and went in. They made everything to order, so he had to wait ten minutes, looking out at Main Street from a table at the front.

Lots of guys his age had girlfriends, but Owen hadn't given it much thought until school started this year.

Four girls from his grade walked past with makeup and highlighted hair and pierced ears and cool clothing, looking like they were in high school. Three guys his age trailed behind in backward baseball caps and ragged sweatshirts and untied sneakers. They didn't notice Owen.

His order came and he started on the huge mound of fries, dipping them one by one in a little paper cup of ketchup. Then he stacked several fries on his hamburger and finished that before it got cold.

Sophie was very nice to him. She believed that he'd been dancing with Charity. She knew the Chase Tavern was haunted, too. And she'd hung back with him last night while trick-or-treating, letting the others get away.

He'd forgotten to get a drink. He wanted Sprite; his mother would be thrilled if he got an orange juice instead. He was thirsty enough to get both and had just enough money, so he did.

Maybe Sophie did actually like him as more than a friend. In some ways, that was scarier than meeting up with a ghost.

The music in the background was a Frank Sinatra CD. "The Way You Look Tonight" had just ended and "Fly Me to the Moon" was starting. In the evenings this place played classic rock, but what was on now was mostly for the cooks.

He drank half of the bottle of juice, then carefully poured in the Sprite and shook it up gently.

What was wrong with just being friends anyway?

Ida Gilman stood next to the horses, unable to step into the carriage.

"We must be on our way," Henry said sternly. "It's over now."

But Ida pleaded for one last visit to the fifth barn. It was the only one that wasn't sealed by bricks. She'd stood outside each of the other four for several minutes that morning, saying good-bye to her children.

"Just one more minute," Ida said. "Please come with me."

The coach held only a few of their possessions; the rest had been sold or left in the house. The trip to Winchendon would take three hours, and Henry was eager to leave Cheshire Notch behind. He shook his head but stepped down.

The ground in the barn had been smoothed and tamped down, showing no sign that a young girl had been buried there. Ida dropped to her knees and prayed.

Henry stood in the doorway. Ida looked up and asked him to come say good-bye. "She was so precious," she whispered.

Henry reluctantly walked over and stood a few feet from the spot. He took off his hat and grunted.

Ida stepped to the front of the barn, reached toward something on the wall, and kept her eyes fixed on Henry's back.

Mason showed up with two chocolate bars, a peanut-butter cup, and a roll of Lifesavers. Owen had already eaten a Mounds bar and a large helping of candy corn, so he went out empty-handed, except for a flashlight.

"How late can you stay?" Owen asked.

"Eleven. You?"

"The same." It was already after nine, but Owen figured the later the better with a haunted house.

He was wearing black jeans, black sneakers, a dark-blue sweatshirt, and a black Windbreaker. Mason had dressed in similar colors, at Owen's urging.

"The barn is the key," Owen said as they walked toward Main Street. "Someone is buried there."

He told Mason the rumors and about the partial foundation of another barn. "I think there are at least two ghosts in the tavern, and one of them's evil. Maybe they spend most of their time in the barn."

"Why would any ghost stay in a barn when they could be in the tavern?" Mason asked.

"Maybe because that's where their bodies are."

The tavern's grounds were very dark tonight, but Owen didn't flick on his light until they were inside the barn. He shined it briefly toward the far wall, identifying a wooden ladder that led straight up to the loft.

"Come on," he said. "Up there."

The loft was a flat wooden platform that covered about a third of the barn. It had no rails, so Mason and Owen sat with their legs hanging over the edge, nine feet above the floor. An old metal bucket and a shovel handle with no blade were the only items up there.

"Just wait," Owen whispered.

They waited a long time. The barn was dusty and the cold air was damp, but Owen kept his eyes fixed on the floor. Even in the pitch dark, his vision adjusted enough that he could see the contours of the barn, but it was too dark to see any details.

Owen nudged Mason hard when he crinkled a candy bar wrapper.

"I'm hungry," Mason said.

"Too bad."

Owen's mind drifted. What if Charity hadn't been killed? She would have died of old age long ago, probably in the 1940s or '50s. Her great-grandchildren would be older than Owen, maybe even older than his parents.

A very faint glow seemed to be coming from the floor toward the back of the barn. It was shapeless and small. Owen felt his muscles tense. He held his breath.

A feeble sound, something like a sob, came from the area of the glow. It was a woman, hunched on all fours, her head bowed. They could see the floor through her; she was like a cloud of steam.

"What do we do?" Mason whispered as softly as he could.

"Just watch," Owen said.

A second presence entered the barn, drifting to a spot behind the woman. There was a brief flash of light as she touched the woman's shoulder. It was Charity.

She was not solid, like the last time, but as milky and transparent as the first ghost. She did not speak, but it was obvious that she was trying to comfort the woman, patting her and then kneeling next to her.

Owen put his hand over his mouth, which was dry and hanging open. He didn't dare blink.

Charity stood and gently tried to coax the woman to come with her. Was it her mother? Owen thought that it must be.

"Charity?" he said softly.

There was no indication that she'd heard him, although he'd said it loud enough that she would.

The woman stayed there. Charity faded and disappeared. The glow gradually grew softer, and then it, too, was gone.

Owen licked his lips. "Wow," he whispered.

"Ghosts," Mason said.

"No kidding."

Mason was nervously drumming his fingers on the floor of the loft. "My legs are shaking," he said. "I don't think I can climb down."

"Just wait," Owen said. "I don't think they'd hurt us."

"How do you know?"

"I've studied up on ghosts, you know. A lot. If there's an evil spirit around here, it sure wasn't them."

They sat without talking for ten more minutes, staring at that space on the floor.

"She was cute," Mason said eventually.

Owen shook his head. "Don't be a jerk. She's dead. Long ago."

"Still cute. Was that her?"

Owen nodded, though he knew Mason couldn't see him. "Yeah," he said. "That was her."

"Call her name again," Mason said. "Maybe she'll come back."

But Owen knew that wouldn't work. The girl he'd danced with had been as real as a live one. What they'd seen tonight was more like a film, an impression of energy that had lingered for so many years.

"Let's go," he said. "Carefully."

The ladder was sturdy but hard to negotiate on the way down, especially in the dark. Owen took a chance and left the flashlight on until they'd both reached the floor.

Owen walked quickly up the dirt pathway toward the street, but a blast of cold air knocked him back. He stumbled and caught himself before he fell. Something like sleet stung his face.

"What was *that?*" Mason said, wiping his eyes with his sleeve.

Owen looked around. Everything was calm. There was very little breeze, nothing natural that could have caused that.

"Henry Gilman," Owen said. "Let's get out of here."

They ran to the street and were a block away before Owen even knew where they were going. He cut across a lawn and onto a walkway that led to the middle of the college.

Ten minutes later they were sprawled on a couch in the student center.

"I don't get it," Mason said. "How can she be two ghosts at once?"

"That's not quite what I'm saying."

The place was quiet; on Saturday nights most students were either out partying or had gone home for the weekend. But the snack bar stayed open until midnight, and Owen and Mason had hustled over here for hot chocolate and cookies.

"Here's how I see it," Owen said. He set his paper cup on a low glass table and leaned forward. He was still shaking, but the hot chocolate was settling him down. "Two types of ghosts. Let's call them *conscious* ghosts and . . . not *un*conscious, but *unaware* ghosts. I've read enough about these things to figure this out. You've got ghosts that are little more than a memory, like a wisp of energy that repeats itself over and over. Probably because of some trauma, or some moment of great impact that was so strong it got captured by the air or something."

Owen took a deep breath and let it out slowly. He pondered his hand, turning it over and spreading his fingers. "Once in a while the energy rebuilds enough that the scene is re-created," he continued. "Like tonight. Who knows why? Electric currents or deep emotions or some other catalyst. And if someone is there at just the right time, they catch a glimpse of that ghost in action again, like you're watching a movie of it. The same moment that happened a hundred years ago, or a thousand."

Mason nodded. "Okay. We've all heard of that."

"Right. So this other form—like Charity the other night at the dance—is this thinking, breathing, *conscious* presence. A 'real' person who's stuck at the age she was back then, right before she died. Not like an image on a film. Not something you just observe, like that woman in the barn tonight. But someone you can actually talk to."

Mason sipped his chocolate and narrowed his eyes. "But

how could Charity be both? She wasn't anything more than an image tonight."

Owen fidgeted and put his foot on the table. "I don't know," he said quickly. "I don't know."

"Maybe when she's with another ghost, she looks like one, too," Mason said. "But she's got enough energy left that she can seem real when she wants to. Like when she wanted to teach you to dance."

Owen sat back and shut his eyes. He felt sorry for Charity. Did she spend her nights trying to calm her grieving mother? Avoiding her horrible father? Had that three-minute dance with Owen been the only bright spot since her death?

He'd go back. Tomorrow night. But not with Mason. Maybe Sophie would sneak back in with him. Sophie understood.

A pack of college students barged through the doors, laughing and talking loudly as they headed to the snack bar. A young woman smiled at Owen as she caught his eye. Her jacket said CHESHIRE NOTCH LACROSSE.

"So, I'm thinking of taking Darla to the movies next Friday," Mason said.

Owen turned and stared at Mason in disbelief. How could he be thinking about something like that? They'd just seen two ghosts!

"You should take Sophie," Mason said.

"You have to *ask*, you know. You don't just decide to take somebody out."

"Yeah," Mason said. "I guess so."

"Shut up about that," Owen said. "Help me think this through. Could what's left of someone be split like that? One repeating image that's separate and stuck, and a real ghost that's . . . aware? And they're independent of each other. It's the same idea that there can be hundreds of photographs or videos of you or me or anybody else, but they aren't really *us* anymore. Just tricks of light and pixels that are left behind while we go forward with our lives."

"Why not?" Mason said.

"Yeah," Owen answered. "Why not?"

He hadn't showered on Saturday, so Owen shouldn't have been surprised that his armpits smelled when he woke up. There'd been a lot of nervous sweat the night before. But he'd never smelled like this before. More like a man than a boy.

He locked the bathroom door and pulled off his T-shirt and leaned close to the mirror with his arms up. Hair.

He'd known it would be growing soon—at least he knew it had better. Mason had hair all over, and some of the kids at school even had the beginning wisps of mustaches. But Owen was skinny and short and didn't look much different than he had in fifth grade. So seeing the armpit hair was a relief. There were only six soft, dark hairs in one pit and four in the other, plus a little more fuzz than he remembered.

He brushed his teeth. His nose looked oily and there was a tiny pink zit under one nostril. He scrubbed his face and toweled dry. Things were changing fast.

His mother wouldn't be happy if he stayed out late another night, especially since there was school tomorrow. But there was too much ghostly energy at the tavern to stay away. It could be years before the elements were right again, and then it would be far too late.

He'd sneak out. He needed to see Charity tonight, while both of them were still the same age.

*   *   *

Henry Gilman had shown only two true emotions in his life: anger and scorn. But as he stood over Charity's makeshift grave, he felt strangely different, if only slightly. He was fleeing this place forever, but perhaps he could linger for a moment.

Henry swallowed hard, then dropped to his knees and closed his eyes.

His wife had taken a heavy, rusty ax from the barn's wall. With four stealthy steps, she silently moved toward her husband, brought back the ax, swung it with all her might, and watched the last of her family drop to the floor, dead.

Within an hour Ida had buried him next to Charity and was on her way. Everyone in Cheshire Notch assumed Henry had fled with his wife. The few in Massachusetts who asked about him were told that he'd gone west by himself to Indiana.

"This is the last time we can sneak in," Sophie said as they walked along Main Street. "It's too risky."

"I know," Owen said.

But Sophie had been very eager when he'd asked her to come with him. She'd slipped out of her house after ten o'clock, just as Owen had done, hoping his mother would assume he was asleep.

The night had turned bitter cold, and a light, icy snow was blowing in their faces.

"I just want to sit in there for a while," Owen said. "See if anything happens."

Sophie smiled. "So, you have a crush on a ghost?"

Owen blushed. "Just curious."

He left the cellar hatch open this time and they felt their way along the wall to the steps. The tavern was dark and eerily quiet, just a steady ticking of a grandfather clock in the parlor where he'd danced with Charity.

They sat on the floor with their backs against the sofa. The tavern wasn't heated, but it wasn't too cold. Every sound and shadow seemed magnified in the gloom.

The tavern's walls were not insulated. Very light cool breezes came from several directions as the wind found its way in.

"Want to go up?" Sophie whispered.

Owen nodded, and they slowly climbed the stairs, stopping to listen at every step.

They sat in the other front bedroom, with its old quilts and rugs and ancient furniture. The fireplace tools glistened in the partial light from the street.

Did a door open and close downstairs? Did Owen hear footsteps? He swallowed hard and felt his skin crawl. His heart was beginning to race.

Then he heard what sounded like gentle humming, like a lilting tune from far away.

"Did you hear that?" he asked.

"Hear what?"

"Nothing." Owen squinted and turned his head to try to hear better.

"Have you ever been upstairs?" Sophie asked.

"We *are* upstairs."

"I mean, way upstairs, in the attic."

"I didn't know there was one."

"It's the spookiest spot in the building," Sophie whispered. "You go up this little staircase, and you're right up there below the roof. It's mostly open space, but there are two rooms that must have been bedrooms way, way back. They're walled off from the rest of the attic. It's incredibly scary up there; I can't imagine sleeping in a spot like that in an old wooden building like this. I mean, if the place caught on fire, you'd have no escape unless you jumped out a window. And it's a long way down."

They sat in silence for several minutes. Owen heard the soft humming again, coming from above. It sent a chill through his chest. "I think she's up there," he squeaked.

Sophie's voice was barely louder than a breath. "She might be."

"Will you go up with me?"

Sophie gave a nervous laugh. "Not at night."

Owen let out his breath; he hadn't even realized he'd been holding it. He felt a few drops of cold sweat drip down his armpits.

"I'm going," he whispered.

Sophie raised her eyebrows. "Be careful."

"I will."

The attic stairs were off a narrow passage between the two back bedrooms. Owen carefully opened the door and shined his flashlight into the space. A dozen wooden steps led to an opening in the floor.

The light caught cobwebs and some broken boards, but the space was dry and musty. Two doors were halfway open. Owen stepped through the doorway to the left and curved his light around the room. He took care not to illuminate the only window, which was the same twelve-paned style as those downstairs.

The space was triangular, as the sloped ceiling followed the sharp angle of the roof and met the floor at the far edge. The wide ceiling boards had been whitewashed but were peeling and looked brittle.

To the side of the window, a simple desktop was attached to the wall—just a thin plank that jutted into the room. A wooden chair sat in front. Among the must and the dust was a very faint aroma of roses.

On the desk was an open diary.

November 2, 1874

Father has been exceptionally angry lately. He swore at Mama today and threatened to hurt her. We are all in mourning still, yet he shows no sadness. He is especially cruel to Jason, my only living brother, and I fear that

The entry ended in midsentence. Owen reached to turn back to a previous page.

More words suddenly appeared, completing the sentence: we are in danger.

Owen jumped back. And as he did, a startled Charity began to take shape, turning toward him.

In a few seconds she seemed as alive as she had at the dance.

"What are you doing here?" she asked.

Owen stared at the ghost and took another step back. "I'm . . . I wanted to see you," he stammered.

"My father would kill you if he found you here."

"Do you know who I am?" he asked.

Charity nodded. "Of course, Owen."

"We danced."

"I remember."

"Are you . . ." Owen hesitated. How do you ask someone if she knows that she's dead? "How long have you lived here?"

"My entire life," Charity replied.

"Right," Owen said. "How long is that?"

"I'm thirteen."

There was a knock on the attic door. "Charity?" came a man's voice.

"Hide!" she whispered.

Owen looked around, frantic. He darted into a dark, dusty alcove, up against the brick chimney. A second later, he heard the man walking up the stairs.

"To whom were you speaking?" the man asked as he entered the room. He sounded annoyed.

"No one, Father," Charity said. "I was just going over my lessons for school."

"You should be asleep," he said. "Come downstairs and go to bed."

"I'll be just a minute," Charity replied. "Let me straighten up my schoolwork."

The man plodded down the stairs without another word.

Charity waited until he was out of earshot. "My father isn't stable," she whispered. "Wait until the house is quiet, then leave without a sound."

Owen crawled out from the alcove. He studied Charity for a moment, fixing her image in his mind. She gave him a puzzled look. "He would throw you through that window without hesitation," she said. Then she turned to leave.

"Charity?" Owen said.

She glanced back.

"Be careful," Owen said, but he knew he couldn't save her. Her death had been many years before.

Owen sat on the floor in the dark. How long should he wait? Was Sophie safe downstairs?

Five minutes, he decided. He let out his breath and tried to calm down.

Owen rubbed his hands together. It was colder up here; the wind found its way with more power through cracks in the boards. He could see his breath in ghostly little wisps. His teeth began to chatter.

He stood and took a tentative step toward the door. And then he heard the attic door open.

The wind, he hoped.

He swallowed hard and took another step.

A stair creaked loudly.

Owen backed into the alcove again and hugged his knees to his chest.

A second stair creaked.

Owen looked around for a weapon, but he saw nothing of use. And he knew he couldn't harm a ghost.

He gripped his flashlight hard.

Another stair creaked. Owen stood and backed tight against the wall.

Perhaps it was Charity, making sure he was all right. But why would she climb so slowly?

He heard soft shuffling in the attic, just outside the room, as if someone in socks was stepping carefully on the floorboards.

He could see the window from the alcove. The ground was far below.

When the door swung open, Owen felt a surge of energy. "Who's there?" he said firmly.

Henry Gilman appeared again, faint and transparent and glowing only slightly. He smelled of smoke and sweat. Owen flicked on the flashlight and shined it at him. The ghost froze.

"Let me out," Owen said.

The ghost looked puzzled by the beam of light, and did not seem to hear what Owen said. In fact, he did not seem aware of Owen at all.

Henry drifted to the window and gazed out. Owen walked slowly toward the door, never turning away from the ghost. He kept the flashlight beam trained on him, too, and waited until Henry faded away in what seemed like a cloud of smoke.

Owen shined the light into every corner of the room. "I know it's too late," he said, "but leave your kids alone."

He walked carefully down the stairs and through the bedrooms.

"Sophie?" he called.

"I'm here."

They hustled down to the main floor, then left through the cellar and shut the hatch tight.

"I need to sit down," Owen said. He plopped onto the brick steps that led up to the kitchen. The porch roof had kept the steps mostly dry.

Sophie sat next to him. Owen shut his eyes and shook his head. "Give me a minute," he murmured. He put his hands to his forehead and pressed.

"You're brave," Sophie said. "I hope it was worth it." She patted Owen's arm.

"What did you see?" she asked when they reached the street. There was just enough snow to see their footprints, like a dusting of flour on the sidewalk.

"A lot."

"Like what?"

He told her about the two ghosts and what Charity had been writing in her diary. "I know she's been dead for more than a century, but I hate that she'll probably die again soon."

"Over and over."

"I hope not. But her afterlife isn't very happy. She's sad and afraid all the time."

"I guess you'll have to visit her again."

The wide Main Street had little traffic at this hour, but Owen stepped into the shadows behind a tree when a car went past.

"I think that was the last diary entry she ever wrote," Owen said. "The book was empty after that. She must have died a short time later."

"Sad," Sophie said.

Sophie lived over on Water Street, past the post office and the public housing buildings. The front porch light was on, and one upstairs.

"Think you'll be in trouble?" Owen asked.

"If they hear me come in."

"Me too. But my mother's probably asleep."

Sophie took a deep breath and smiled, looking toward her yard. "I'll tiptoe," she said, and she giggled.

Owen started to walk away.

"Owen?"

"Yeah?"

"Mason's taking Darla to the movies on Friday."

"Is he?"

"Yeah." She waited, then shrugged and began to walk.

Owen shoved his hands into his pockets and found his voice. "Want to go, too?"

She nodded and said yeah. And then she slipped away into the darkness.

Owen's house was dark, as he had hoped. It meant that his mother had gone to bed. If she'd known he was missing, she'd have every light on and would have called Mason's house.

This was good. Another hour wouldn't mean a thing. He stayed on back streets until he was near the tavern, then ran across Main when no cars were in sight.

Tree branches rattled in the wind and the grass had a slick dusting of snow. He didn't dare go back inside the tavern. Too scary, and too illegal. When Sophie was along, he'd felt that it was almost okay to go in because of her grandmother's connection to the historical society and all.

He knew better. It was wrong to go in there.

But if that diary was still on the desk? Would it provide any information?

Owen took a deep breath. He had to know.

He knew the way through the cellar now and crossed quickly to the steps. He held the kitchen door firmly so it wouldn't squeak, then paused to gaze at the hearth. He dropped to his knees.

Charity had lived here. She'd been a living, breathing girl for thirteen years. He was thirteen, too. He couldn't imagine his life ending for many, many decades. So much ahead; so much to think and to do and enjoy.

He climbed the two sets of stairs, shaking as he ascended into the attic. The house was quiet save for the ticking and the wind. No signs of ghosts, just dust and spiderwebs and chilled dry air.

He stopped outside the room with the desk and listened for humming or footsteps.

His hand trembled as he pushed the door open. He closed it behind him, just in case.

The desk was empty. He shined his light on the floor and around the corners of the room, but there was no sign that anyone had been in here lately. There was an undisturbed layer of dust on the desk and the chair.

Owen sat at the desk for a few minutes anyway, imagining what it had been like to live here in fear. This room must have been Charity's oasis, a place away from her father's fury and her mother's grief. A place to write and to hum and to look out the window at the trees.

As he stood to leave the attic, he noticed a dark item hanging from the back of the door. He winced when his light revealed what it was.

He took the tricornered hat from the hook. The Walmart sticker confirmed that it was his.

He held the hat to his face and inhaled. Was there a slight hint of Charity? He wasn't sure. He hung it back on the hook. Maybe it would make some kind of difference.

It was snowing again when Owen reached the yard, but the wind had eased and the flakes were soft and fluffy. A police car drove by, headed for the highway.

Owen waited until the car was out of sight before sprinting across Main Street toward home.

This book developed during a time of transition. The idea came to fruition under my longtime editor Joan Slattery, who took her career in a new direction a few years ago. Allison Wortche and Nancy Hinkel guided me for an interim period, and Michele Burke saw the book through to publication. I'm indebted to you all!

Thanks to the Cheshire County Historical Society in Keene, New Hampshire, for access to the Wyman Tavern, my model for the Chase in this book. Often, late at night, I walk past the tavern and think I catch glimpses of spirits in the windows. Keene inspires me, with its cemeteries and its Pumpkin Festival, its historical aura and its quirky New England charms.

RICH WALLACE is the author of many books for children and teenagers, including *Wrestling Sturbridge, Sports Camp,* and the Kickers series. He lives in New Hampshire with his wife, novelist Sandra Neil Wallace. You can visit his website at richwallacebooks.com.